W9-BYH-173

FOR REVIEW ONLY
SMITH PUBLICITY, INC.
856-489-8654

CREATED EQUAL

CREATED EQUAL

A NOVEL

R.A. BROWN

TATE PUBLISHING & Enterprises

Published by Tate Publishing & Enterprises, LLC
127 E. Trade Center Terrace | Mustang, Oklahoma 73064 USA
1.888.361.9473 | www.tatepublishing.com

Tate Publishing is committed to excellence in the publishing industry. The company reflects the philosophy established by the founders, based on Psalm 68:11,
"The Lord gave the word and great was the company of those who published it."

Book design copyright © 2011 by Tate Publishing, LLC. All rights reserved.
Cover design by Amber Gulilat
Interior design by Kellie Southerland

Published in the United States of America

ISBN: 978-1-61346-579-0
1. Fiction / Legal   2. Fiction / Thrillers
11.04.15

CHAPTER ONE

As Tommy finished the last sip of his coffee, he neatly folded the Wall Street Journal and tossed it in the recycle bin. Dutifully he rinsed out his cup and put it in the dishwasher, a reflection of all those years Luisa had instructed him on being tidy. He went into the bathroom, brushed his teeth, and combed his hair. It was still quite thick, and he wore it parted on the right side with a little fringe over ears. The back was neatly trimmed, but just long enough to barely touch the back of his collar. The reddish blond hair of his youth had turned, not silver, not gray, but pure white. It was a stark contrast to his dark complexion. As he stared at his reflection, he noticed that his face had very few, if any wrinkles, and he looked younger than his fifty-five years. All those years on the treadmill have paid off, he thought to himself. At six feet, three inches and 195 pounds, he was very fit, with a narrow waist and broad shoulders. When Tommy O'Reilly entered a room, he would invariably attract the attention of women of all ages.

Opening the heavy wooden closet door in his bedroom, he scanned through his immense wardrobe and selected a light gray wool suit. It had been impeccably tailored and emphasized his impressive build.

He paired it with a pink shirt and a light blue silk tie with pink flowers that bespoke of its designer, Hermes. To complete his ensemble, he pulled on a pair of hand made black ostrich boots that felt like a second skin. *Ahh*, he thought, a fine pair boots was one of the many things he had picked up from Joe Bob.

After graduation from law school, Tommy had gone to work for Joe Bob Finely as an associate. Joe Bob was one of the top plaintiff's lawyers in Texas and only took cases when the defendants had lots of money. Products liability, personal injury, women who wanted divorces from their wealthy and sometimes philandering husbands; he took them all.…and sometimes the women too. It was a small law firm with no partners. Only Joe Bob and a small staff of associate lawyers to do the grunt work. There was always endless legal research, motion dockets, preparation of pleadings, and anything else that Job Bob deemed necessary. Almost immediately Tommy began to show the promise that Joe Bob had seen in him. He soon began trying his own lawsuits, and with great success. More importantly, he began to attract his own clients.

Since the Code of Ethics had been liberalized to allow attorneys to advertise, Tommy took full advantage of the change. The fact that he was a native Houstonian, had been a notable football player at University of Houston, and the son of the well-known Paddy O'Reilly had helped him immensely. Ten years and two months after Tommy's graduation from law school, he had become Joe Bob's first and only law partner. It was agreed that they would split fifty-fifty on every thing the firm brought in. Tommy was on a roll.

Joe Bob and Tommy were alike in many ways, but the biggest difference was in their relationships with women. When it came to the "fairer sex," Tommy had no problem finding attractive, available women who were more than willing to spend time with him. Joe Bob was Tommy's equal in attracting women, but the length of their relationships differed greatly. Tommy always found a way to extricate himself from the particular belle of the moment whenever talks began to venture into the area of a long-term future together. Tommy had no desire to engage in marriage, or a relationship of any permanence, for that matter. Perhaps it was due partly to his lack of faith in the old adage "live happily ever after until death do us part."

Joe Bob had no lack of confidence in anything he did. When a beautiful woman with the physical attributes of a Playboy bunny, relatively high intelligence, an entertaining wit, and a rapacious sexual appetite told Joe Bob that her only goal in life was to make him happy forever; his ego gave him no chance but to believe her. That same ego would also not allow him to even consider a prenuptial agreement. No woman who was ever given the opportunity to spend the rest of her life with Joe Bob Finley would even consider changing her mind...or so he thought.

Only after the third Mrs. Finley had done the seemingly impossible and left for greener pastures did Joe Bob have a change of heart. Not only had she kept a significant amount of Joe Bob's considerable community property, but she also took the last of his resolve for a permanent relationship. Accordingly, Joe Bob became a favorite client of the most elite female escort services of Houston. Surprisingly, he found that his relationships were as meaningful as any of those he had with any Mrs. Finley, were considerably less complicated, and a whole lot cheaper too.

It was in the mid '90s that Joe Bob and Tommy's fortunes changed considerably. Perhaps not so much for Joe Bob, but certainly for Tommy. In an act of predilection the heart which Joe Bob had poured out to so many juries, the heart which he had given so carelessly to all the women he thought he loved, suddenly gave out. Joe Bob went as any true Texan male would want to go, in bed with his boots off. When Tommy heard the news, he was duly saddened, but happy in knowing that Joe Bob went engaged in one of the two things he loved the best: trying lawsuits and, well, the other.

At the time of Joe Bob's untimely demise, tobacco litigation had been the focal point all across the country in the States Attorney Generals' offices. Armed with the harmful effects of tobacco and the additional costs of tobacco-related diseases burdening Medicaid plans, the states began to seek recourse from tobacco companies. The Attorney General of Texas began the process of interviewing plaintiff's trial lawyers in search of the best in the state to pursue action against the large tobacco companies. Five lawyers were selected to file the action in Texarkana, Texas, a well-known jurisdiction for rendering higher than normal monetary judgments on behalf of plaintiffs.

Under the arrangement, the lawyers were to bear all expenses and would have a contingency fee based upon their success. After three years of litigation and the plaintiff's lawyers having spent over thirty million dollars of their own money, the state of Texas received an award in excess of 17 billion dollars. The five lawyers were awarded additional fees from the tobacco companies of 3.3 billion dollars. Three other states also received judgments against the tobacco companies, but unlike Texas, the attorneys' fees were in the millions, not billions. Shortly after the Texas decision, forty-six other states settled with the tobacco companies in an amount exceeding 200 billion dollars overall, which at the time was the largest transfer of wealth in the nation's history.

Joe Bob and Tommy's firm had not been named in the elite group that became known as the Tobacco Five. When faced with the substantial costs of bringing and continuing the lawsuit with questionable outcome, one of Joe Bob's old law school classmates, who was one of the Five, decided to bring in another firm to share the costs. He approached Joe Bob and Tommy about joining forces to share in the expenses for an equal share of the upside.

Since the tobacco companies had only lost two cases that had been filed for related diseases in the United States, the odds were long. Joe Bob was used to long odds, because that was what a plaintiff's trial lawyer's life was all about. A loss meant nothing, but a win, well, that's why God made contingency fees. They went for half and hit the jackpot. Unfortunately, wherever Joe Bob was he would not enjoy any of it, and Tommy had more money than he could ever spend in a lifetime.

CHAPTER TWO

After dressing, Tommy picked up the telephone and called down to the lobby. "Good morning, George. Will you please have the Navigator brought to the front?"

"Yes sir, Mr. O'Reilly. Right away, sir!"

Tommy had purchased the Lincoln Navigator the previous year when the US government had bailed out General Motors and Chrysler. Since Ford didn't need any of his or other taxpayers' dollars, he felt he would reward them by driving a Ford product and had traded in his German-made luxury car the day after the bailout. That was the way with Tommy O'Reilly. If something made sense to him, he just did it.

It was the same type of reasoning that had caused him to form the O'Reilly Law Group. After the tobacco payout, he didn't need to work for money anymore. He wanted to work; or maybe he needed to work because he enjoyed the law and trying lawsuits. He had entrusted his fortune to Peter James, a high school football teammate and one of his longtime friends. Peter had received his MBA in finance from the Wharton school of business and was very astute in the investments market. He stimulated the growth of Tommy's investment income such that it greatly exceeded his personal needs.

It occurred to Tommy that there were countless people who were financially unable to have decent legal representation when the need arose. He could afford to help these people without pay, pro bono work. It made sense, and from that thought, the O'Reilly Law Group was born. Tommy sought out and hired the best and brightest attorneys to handle legal work for any client who was unable to afford the fees of comparable legal representation. With that all in place as Tommy drove to his office on a beautiful spring day in Houston, he felt a surge of contentment with his life and all that it afforded him.

Tommy wheeled the big Navigator into the parking lot adjacent to the three-story office building he had purchased and completely remodeled when he opened his law firm. It was in downtown Houston on South Main Street, and its only tenants were the associate lawyers, paralegals, and the support staff for the O'Reilly Law Group. It was also conveniently located right next to the Metro line, which allowed an easy train ride to other parts of the city. Most of the attorneys, however, used Manuel, Joe Bob's former driver, whom Tommy had kept on staff for the firm to go to courthouses and attorney's offices. Tommy didn't believe in chancing any of his associates being late for court or mediation because of a train schedule delay or having to walk in a Houston rainstorm. But the metro was very convenient for their clients who, for the most part, had very little means.

Betty Lincoln, with a cup of coffee in one hand and a file folder in the other, greeted Tommy with her ever-present radiant smile as he entered the reception area of his offices. She was exceptionally pretty, although heavyset and somewhat matronly in appearance. Her flawless, mocha-colored skin was set off by sparkling enormous brown eyes. And when she smiled, her teeth were a neon white, almost unimaginable. She wore her dark, curly hair in a neat, short haircut with a few straggling strands of gray starting to sprout through.

"Good morning, boss," Betty said, still smiling at him as she took her seat behind her ornate desk facing the door. "You look mighty chipper this morning, boss; what gives?"

"Why shouldn't I be?" he chimed back. "It's one of those remarkable spring days that we live for in Houston, and the Astros are breaking spring training with the new season starting next week. I think this may be our year."

"You say that every year, boss, and every year they wind up last in their division." Betty teased. "What makes you think the Astros will be any different this year?"

"Right now we're tied for first place, Betty. Please get me two tickets for opening night. You know the ones in the first row behind our dugout?"

"Right now you're also tied for last," she rejoined, rolling her eyes, "but two tickets it is. After all, it's your money and your time. I hope you have some pretty thing to take so it won't be a total waste."

"A total waste of time would be taking some woman to a ball game, Betty." Tommy smiled. "What's on my schedule today?"

"Willis Thompson wants to meet with you about a potential new client he talked to yesterday afternoon. You also have a meeting with Aleksandra Kowalski and Gerald Grant wants you to review an appellate brief before he files it. It's due today." She read from her notes, which Tommy knew she had already memorized.

"Who is Aleksandra Kowalski?" Tommy inquired.

"She's a potential new client Don Stoop referred. She asked to speak to you specifically."

Stoop was the head lawyer of the local ACLU and periodically would refer clients who, although deserving of representation, the ACLU could not handle because the particular situation of the client did not fit the ACLU charter.

"Okay. Let me work on the brief. When Mrs. Kowalski arrives, I'll meet with her, and then I will deal with Thompson and his potential new client. Is the coffee fresh?"

"It's *Miss* Kowalski, not *Mrs.* Kowalski, boss, and I will announce her when she gets here," Betty pointedly said, ignoring his reference to the coffee, a not-too-subtle hint that she had better things to do than to keep track of his coffee.

Tommy grinned and said, "Yes, ma'am," and made his way to the coffee bar.

CHAPTER THREE

Tommy was engrossed in the appellate brief and was making notes in the margin when his phone rang.

"Ms. Kowalski is here to see you, boss."

"Thank you, Betty, I'll be right out," he said.

Tommy went out the door to the reception area to meet Aleksandra Kowalski. Tommy was immediately struck by her wholesome and fresh appearance. She was of medium height, maybe five feet and six inches tall, with auburn hair complemented by amber yellow highlights. Her skin was fair. She wore no makeup except for a light shade of lipstick that matched the color of her hair. Her eyes were green, a deep green, like three-carat emeralds with the dark iris in the middle. To cap it off, she had a splash of freckles on her cheeks.

"Hello," he said, smiling. "I'm Tommy O'Reilly." He took her hand to shake it and found that it was soft, smooth, and cool.

She looked back at him and said, "Hello, Mr. O'Reilly, I'm Aleksandra Kowalski," with a smile that was as bright as her eyes.

As he led her into his office he noted that the green dress she had on, though not tight or revealing, could not conceal a trim and athletic figure. Tommy sat her down in the leather chair in front of his desk and went behind the desk to take his own seat. Tommy had never been married but had never lacked for female companionship. As he had gotten older, he had instituted a rule of self-discipline that he called his "daughter rule." Simply put, he would never date anyone who was young enough to be his daughter if he had one or any woman who was more than twenty years his junior. In his thirties, his daughter rule had not been an issue, but in his forties it had become more problematic. Now in his midfifties, his rule of self-restraint would eliminate any lady the age of thirty-five or less. He thought Aleksandra Kowalski would be off-limits, but just barely.

After she declined coffee and a soft drink, Tommy asked her, "How may I help you, Miss Kowalski? It is Miss, and not Mrs.?"

"Yes, it is Miss Kowalski. I'm not married. Are you married, Mr. O'Reilly?"

"No, I'm not," he answered.

"Have you ever been married, Mr. O'Reilly?" she asked.

"No, I haven't," he said.

"Are you Catholic, Mr. O'Reilly?"

"Why all the questions, Miss Kowalski?" Tommy asked.

"I think it's important to know you better before I decide whether to engage your services," she replied.

Tommy looked at her and said, "First of all, no one engages this firm. All of the work we do for clients is pro bono."

"Then I hope your clients get more value than what they pay for, Mr. O'Reilly," she grinned.

Aleksandra has a sense of humor, Tommy thought. He chuckled and said, "So far no complaints."

"May I continue with my questions, Mr. O'Reilly?" she asked.

O'Reilly nodded his head. "If you wish."

"Well then, are you Catholic? With an Irish name, I think you might be," she said.

"Yes. My deceased father was Irish Catholic, and my mother is Italian and still living. I did not have a choice in the matter. They made the choice for me."

"Are you a practicing Catholic, Mr. O'Reilly?" she continued.

"Ms. Kowalski, I don't wish to be rude, but what does my religion or lack thereof have to do with anything?" O'Reilly asked.

"Because I wish to sue the Catholic Church," she said firmly, "and I want to know if you would have a conflict of interest."

"Ms. Kowalski, this firm, as a matter of principle, does not represent supposed victims of pedophilia by Catholic priests. And before you ask, it has nothing to do with my religion. More often than not, cases today tend to be more based in fraud than in fact. Oftentimes a Catholic adult will read that a priest she or he knew in their young years has been accused as a pedophile. Some see this as an opportunity for big bucks. It really becomes a question of the Catholic adult saying one thing and the priest another, and the priest is behind the eight ball. If someone is truly traumatized by something, which I agree is truly horrific, I question their true motive at this late date and wonder why they did not bring this up years ago."

"No, Mr. O'Reilly, I'm not here because I had a sexual encounter with a priest." She blushed.

"Well, if you're not a victim of pedophilia, then what has the Catholic Church done to you that you believe is the basis of a lawsuit?" Tommy asked.

"Mr. O'Reilly, I'm here because I want you to represent me," she said determinedly. "I want to sue the Catholic Church to allow me to enter the seminary so that I may become a priest!"

CHAPTER FOUR

Tommy was seldom at a loss for words, but this time he was taken aback, and he stammered, "Miss Kowalski—"

She interrupted him and said demurely, "Please call me Alex."

"Okay, Alex it is, and everybody calls me Tommy," O'Reilly replied.

"Mr. O'Reilly, if it's okay with you, I prefer to call you Mr. O'Reilly."

"Whatever you wish, Alex," Tommy said in exasperation, "but you can't become a priest!"

"And just why not?" she responded angrily.

"Why not?" Tommy asked incredulously. "*Why not* is because you are a woman, or at least I think you are."

"Yes, I am a woman, and that is precisely why I am here in your law office. Don't the laws of this country provide equal opportunity for women and men alike? Are there not laws in this country that prevent unjust discrimination against women based solely upon their gender? I am a woman in this country. The Catholic Church is an institution in this country. Is it not required to abide by the laws of this country? How can it legally discriminate against me solely because of my sex?" she asked heatedly.

Tommy took a deep breath while collecting his thoughts and then calmly said, "Yes, there are laws that prohibit discrimination against women. However, the First Amendment to the Bill of Rights of the United States Constitution clearly defines that there will be a separation between church and state in this country. That precludes United States laws from intervening into the activities of a church. A church has the right to practice its religion as it chooses."

"I understand that," Alexandra responded. "But the same Constitution and Bill of Rights that requires the separation of church and state also requires the separation between the executive, legislative, and judicial branches of the government. Yet in the last forty years there has been a president in the *executive* branch that was forced to resign because he violated laws enacted by the *legislative* branch and another president in the *executive* branch who was impeached by the *legislative* branch. Where is the separation of the executive branch and the legislative branch there? If the president of the United States is not exempt from the laws of this country, how can any church be exempt? Also, the Supreme Court, the highest institution of the *judicial* branch inserted itself into the *legislative* process and elected a president by a five to four decision. It's clear that the law and the courts established to enforce that law are paramount in this country over the separation of the executive, legislative, and judicial branches. How can the church hide behind the separation of church and state when their actions are likewise clearly a violation of United States law?"

"You've done your homework well, Alex." Tommy grinned and said, "Are you sure you wouldn't rather be a lawyer?"

"Please don't humor me, Mr. O'Reilly. When the laws of this country clearly state that no one can discriminate against a woman solely because of her gender, how can the Catholic Church do what it does? God has called *me*, not me as a *woman*, but me as a *person* to the vocation of the priesthood," she said.

Tommy took out a legal pad and pen and said, "Perhaps we should start at the beginning," and he began to write down as she talked.

"I was born here in Houston thirty-three years ago. My father and mother were very religious Polish Catholics and raised me and my four brothers and three sisters in the Catholic Church. We attended mass at St. Peter and Paul, and I went there to parochial school from kindergarten to the eighth grade. After that I went to St. Gwendolyn High School and graduated valedictorian of my class." Then she grinned and said, "But since it is an all girls' school and I didn't compete against any boys, maybe you're not so impressed."

Tommy looked up at her smiling face and said, "Impressive nonetheless. Please continue."

"I received an academic scholarship from St. Louis University, the Jesuit school in Missouri, and received an undergraduate degree in theology and a doctorate in Trinity Studies," she continued.

Tommy interrupted and grinned. "There are boys at St. Louis University. Did you graduate valedictorian there?"

"Just in undergraduate school," she said demurely.

He chuckled with embarrassment. "Okay, please continue."

"The faith that my parents instilled in me is the core of my life. I am not interested in men or any type of a social life. I teach religion at St. Gwendolyn and attend Mass and communion every day and read the Bible and books of Christian scholars," she said.

"Mr. O'Reilly, I want you to know this is not a whim or fancy. I have prayed months and months over this decision, and God has given me his answer. In my heart I know he wants me to be a priest. And I will be a good priest with his help. I know I have to do this, and he has led me to you for your help. Please believe me, everything I have told you, and you can investigate everything I have told you, it's all true. I'm an excellent candidate for the priesthood. The only thing, and I mean the only thing, I don't have in the way of qualifications in the church's eyes, is the lack of male genitals. I ask you, why is the presence of a penis a fundamental requirement for the priesthood?"

Tommy shrugged his shoulders and said, "I don't know."

"I don't know either," she continued. "All priests take a vow of celibacy when they enter the priesthood. Since a priest may not have sex, what does a priest's sex have to do with the role of a priest? So what difference does it make what sex organs a priest has? If I had a sex operation, changed my gender, would the church then say I'm better qualified than I am now? Why is there a condition for priesthood that has absolutely no relevance to what makes a good priest? Spirituality, desire to help others, and the dedication to do God's work here on earth is what makes a good priest. I assure you that I have those qualifications."

"Have you actually considered that?" Tommy asked.

"Considered what, Mr. O'Reilly?" Alex answered.

"Have you considered a sex change operation," Tommy responded. "We have represented a number of transgender individuals referred to us by gay organizations we help out and had them legally declared to be a sex opposite from the one they were born with. Off the top of my head, and again purely from a legal standpoint, I believe you might have a better chance in your action if you were declared legally a male. If you are legally a male, I believe your chances would be greatly enhanced."

"Consider a sex change operation? Of course I haven't. I would never do such a thing! That's exactly the hypocrisy of the Catholic Church that I'm talking about! So if I emasculate myself and add a piece of anatomy that has nothing to do with being a priest, I have a better chance of being a priest? Don't you see how ludicrous that is?" Alex pleaded.

Tommy stared at Alex for what seemed like a long time, and her gaze never wavered from his. She was both honest and endearing, and he was impressed by her zeal. But it was time to dig in.

Tommy cleared his throat and said, "Alex, I believe you're sincere in what you've told me. But have you thought about what will happen if you file this lawsuit against the Catholic Church? The church has enormous resources, maybe more than any other institution in the world. They will immediately begin to research every aspect of your life. Your parents, your brothers and sisters, and your friends will all be involved in that process. Are you ready for that? Are you ready for all those you love, for their lives and their relationships, to be put under a microscope? The church will try to find out everything they can to show that you are neither passionate nor serious about what you want.

"If you are a private person," he continued, "and I suspect you are, prepare yourself for a firestorm of publicity by the news people. They also will dig to find any dirt they can. They love to do that so they can scoop the other news outlets. Expect to see some boy you barely know on cable news telling a talking head that you were the greatest lay he ever had. It'll be a lie, but he'll get his fifteen minutes of fame. You could sue for slander, but what good would it do you? Please make no mistake about this. It'll be a lawsuit that the Catholic Church cannot afford to lose. No way! To lose this lawsuit would put one of their most historic and sacred teachings at total risk, not only in the United States but worldwide. Are you ready for this, Alex?"

"I'm not afraid, Mr. O'Reilly. Are you afraid?"

"I'm not afraid for me, Alex, because no one can really harm me. But I am afraid for you. I want to be sure that if we file this lawsuit, we have legal standing to do so and that we have a fighting chance to win. To do otherwise is not representing your best interests."

He turned his chair and stared out the window. After a moment of deliberation he turned back to her and said, "So I want to do some research and think about what we've discussed. This being Friday, I have the rest of the day and the weekend, and that should be enough time. Where can I reach you on Monday?"

"I am living with two nuns, Sister Mary Caroline and Sister Agnes. Their ministry is at Mercy Hospital, and the hospital provides them a house near the medical center. I went to high school with both of them, and they are very good friends of mine." She gave him the telephone number of the house.

"Have you talked to your friends about your decision?" Tommy inquired.

"Yes, I have, and Sister Mary Caroline heartily supports my goal, but Sister Agnes vehemently does not," she answered.

Tommy chuckled and said, "An opinion poll from people who are very knowledgeable on the issue splits fifty-fifty. It could be worse." He smiled. "I'll walk you to the door."

Tommy opened the front door of his offices, which led to the outside, and they stood a moment.

Tommy turned to her and said, "Good-bye, Alex. You've given me a lot to think about. I'll be in touch with you on Monday."

He stuck out his hand to say good-bye when she looked deep into his eyes and said, "Thank you, Mr. O'Reilly. You're not alone in your decision, you know." Then she turned and began gazing at the parking lot. Slowly she turned back to face him and said quietly, "God will be with you every step of the way. He will guide you in your deliberations this weekend. Whatever decision you make will be the right one."

Her absolute conviction in God was so evident that Tommy wondered if he could ever have a conviction about anything the way she did.

"If he's going to be with me, then I hope he's prepared for a lot of heavy overtime." He smiled. They shook hands and said good-bye, and Tommy closed the door and stepped back into the reception area.

CHAPTER FIVE

As Tommy walked back into the reception area, Betty was at her desk with her face framing a Cheshire grin.

"You're a man in God's hands? I guess there has to be a first time for everything," she said, stifling a giggle.

"How would you know it's the first time?" He growled.

"My, my," she said. "What happened to Mr. Chipper? You know, a 'great spring day and the Astros starting with hope springing eternal' and all of that stuff?"

"I have a lot of things on my mind now that I didn't before. By the way, cancel those baseball tickets. I don't think I'll be in a position to use them."

"No can do, boss, they're signed, sealed, and delivered into my competent and somewhat elegant hands."

"Well then give them to Leroy and Benjamin."

Leroy was Betty's husband, and Benjamin was their youngest child, a junior in high school and still at home, their older two children having left to pursue degrees at college. Leroy was the total opposite of Betty in physical appearance. Where Betty tended to be on the heavy side, Leroy was about the same height as Betty and thin as a rail. Since Betty had an income that more than provided them a comfortable lifestyle, Leroy had taken on the traditional duties of a homemaker early in their marriage. He maintained the house, did the chores, and did all of the cooking. In fact, his barbecued, crispy, baby-back pork ribs were the best that Tommy had ever tasted. While Betty had maintained her maiden name of Lincoln, Leroy used his surname of Williams. Tommy thought it was just a matter of time until Leroy adopted the name Williams-Lincoln or Lincoln-Williams. But one thing was for sure, Betty and Leroy were very happy as a married couple.

"What makes you think that Leroy and Benjamin would want to waste their time watching the Astros?" Betty asked. "They can stay at home and get something more exciting on the Nature Channel like watching cows graze."

"Maybe, just maybe, Betty, they might enjoy a night away from *you*," Tommy replied.

"Hmmm. Spoken just like someone who has never experienced the joys of marital bliss. Okay, I'll take them home, and they can have them, assuming the dog doesn't eat them first." In spite of himself, Tommy smiled. "Okay, now that that's finally settled, I need to speak to Silk."

"As I had mentioned to you earlier, boss, Willis also wants to speak to you about a potential new client," Betty responded.

"Okay. If he's available, please send him in."

Tommy went into his office, followed a minute later by Willis Thompson. Willis "Silk" Thompson was a striking African American male with skin the color of light chocolate, set off by expressive and brown eyes, a straight nose, and a great smile that he could use to his advantage. He was tall, three inches taller than Tommy, with a slim athletic build, broad in the shoulders and narrow at the waist and hips. He moved with the grace of an athlete, which he most certainly had been and probably still was if he ever was inclined to do so again. Tommy thought he reminded him of a younger version of Denzel Washington. He had the same melodious timber to his voice, and, besides being younger, he was more handsome, if that could be possible.

CHAPTER SIX

When Willis Thompson walked into Tommy's office he noticed that Tommy was staring out the window, which Tommy often did when he was deep in thought. He stood there for a moment, and when Tommy didn't turn around, Willis cleared his throat. The sound broke Tommy out of his reverie, and he turned around to face him.

"Oh, sorry, Silk. I was lost in thought," Tommy said.

"You sure were," Willis replied.

Anything to do with the lady who just left?" Willis inquired.

"Yes it does, Silk," Tommy replied.

Willis was "Silk" to Tommy because of his background. At his first day of basketball practice at the University of Texas, Willis was guarded by an upper classman. Willis went to his left on the dribble, bounced the ball behind his back as to if to go to his right, took one step, and bounced the ball between his legs in a cross-over move that left the upper classman waving at him as Willis passed him by to the basket. He went up and laid the ball in, not dunking as he could have done, but not wanting to show anyone up, particularly a teammate. There was silence for a moment, and then the other players yelled the customary congratulatory phrases accompanied with the requisite high fives. The Texas coach merely said, "That was as smooth as silk. Yes siree bob, as smooth as silk." And from that day on in Texas athletic circles, Willis and "Silk" were synonymous.

Tommy continued, "Her name is Aleksandra Kowalski, and Ms. Kowalski wants to sue the Catholic Church."

"I thought we had a policy of not bringing action against the Catholic Church."

"No, we have a policy of not representing alleged victims of sexual abuse by priests. I have told you my reasons for that before. This is different," Tommy answered.

"How so?" Willis asked.

"Big difference, Silk. Aleksandra Kowalski wants to be a priest," said Tommy.

There was silence for a long moment as Willis stared at Tommy. Finally Willis stammered, "She can't be a priest, Tommy. She's a woman, for God's sake!"

"Exactly. And it's also for God's sake that she wants to be a priest and take on the Catholic Church to allow her to do so. Believe me. She firmly believes that God is asking her to do this."

Tommy thought a moment and then said, "Before we decide to take her case, let's start with due diligence first. I want you to contact Tim Prentice and see if he can start an immediate investigation on Ms. Kowalski." Tim Prentice, a former FBI agent, was the best private investigator in Houston and had a very proficient team who uncovered the secret life that Tommy felt most, if not all, people had.

"And it needs to be done by Monday morning," Tommy instructed.

Tommy passed over all of the information he had jotted down in his conversation with Alex, which included her social security number, the schools she attended, present and former addresses, and the like. "This will get him started, and tell Tim to approach this as if she were a witness in a crucial case that we'd have to cross-examine about her lifestyle. Also talk to Billie Sullivan and Rickie Bush," Tommy said.

Billie and Rickie were female lawyers who joined the firm after graduating in the top 10 percent of their law school classes. The firm afforded them the flexible hours to be married, raise a family, and still utilize their expertise in legal research. In today's electronic legal world, Billie and Rickie were equally effective on the computer at home or at the office.

"Have them research the issues for a case like this. The Catholic Church has the First Amendment on their side, which clearly states that there's a separation of church and state and that the government is prohibited from interfering into church affairs. On the other hand, there is the Civil Rights Act of 1964, which prohibited discrimination of women without justifiable cause for employment. I remember that the act specifically excluded churches and their employees. But we are in the twenty-first century, and 1964 was a while ago. I know there have been court cases that have expanded the rights of women. Have Billie and Rickie get together and divide areas of research. And by Monday morning, I want to know if the United States Federal Court, Southern District of Texas has appropriate jurisdiction and venue to hear this case. Silk, this is very important. I want to know if we can get this case past a motion for summary judgment and get the case to a jury. If we have any legal standing at all, I want to know."

Tommy felt totally comfortable turning all the legal research over to Silk, who was the smartest person Tommy had ever met. While playing basketball at the University of Texas, he had graduated in three years with a 4.0 average in history with a minor in African American studies. With a year of athletic eligibility left, he had taken the LSAT and passed with flying colors. He enrolled in UT law school as a freshman while playing his senior year of basketball, a feat nobody could remember having been accomplished at Texas before. Two years later, he had graduated first in a class of 282.

"Tommy, surely you haven't decided to take this on?"

"No, I haven't made a decision, but let's get through the practical and legal due diligence first. I'll work through some other issues I've thought about over the weekend," Tommy said.

"Tommy, is our potential client for real?" Willis asked.

"I really think so, Silk. I really do. But let's see what Tim and his interviewers and computer techno-nerds find out," Tommy said.

A long silence ensued with each in his own thoughts, after which Tommy asked, "What about the new client that you wanted to discuss?"

"It'll keep," Willis replied. "I need to get started on this," he said as he got up to leave.

As Willis reached the door Tommy said, "Oh, by the way, did you know a recent poll said that Catholic nuns were split down the middle on whether women should be priests?"

"No, I didn't know that," Willis said, turning around. "Is it relevant?"

"Not really," Tommy answered, "but I was just thinking, Joe Bob would take fifty-fifty anytime."

CHAPTER SEVEN

Tommy went through the rest of his day taking calls, talking to associates, reading briefs, and all the assorted tasks that the head of the largest pro bono firm in the fourth largest city in the country would deal with. The organizations that referred clients to the O'Reilly Law Group were numerous. They included Alcoholics Anonymous, Al-Anon, Aliteen, organizations that helped unmarried pregnant women, those who help battered women, and essentially all the charitable organizations in Houston. People seeking charitable help often needed legal assistance and obviously were too poor to afford it. Those people would be referred to the O'Reilly Law Group, who would gladly assist them, but it made for many and wildly varied legal issues. He was glad when the day was over. He left the office, got into his Lincoln Navigator, and drove to Towers of Houston, a twenty-five-story luxury inner-city high rise that abutted the south side of the green and expansive Hermann Park adjacent to the medical center. He tossed the keys to the porter and took the elevator to his apartment.

After changing into shorts and a t-shirt, Tommy went into his kitchen and took out a prime New York strip steak, one of a shipment he had regularly sent in from the Wooden Nickel. While it marinated, he sliced a potato into wedges and seasoned them and put a head of lettuce in the freezer. Then he poured a healthy amount of Black Bushmill's Irish whiskey into a tumbler over ice as a cocktail before dinner, a habit he had no doubt inherited from his Irish father, Paddy. He took a Cusano eighteen-year double Connecticut cut cigar from his humidor and went outside. It was a beautiful night; the type of night that if Houston had 365 nights out of the year instead of 220, the city fathers would have to issue immigration visas to control the influx of people. His apartment had terraces on all four sides, and he chose the one facing west. Houston being flat, the lights stretched as far as he could see. As he clipped his cigar, lit it, and took a sip of Black Bush, he pondered on the fate of one Alex Kowalski.

A second Black was finished as well as his cigar, and Tommy went into the kitchen and pulled a bottle of Titus Cabernet, opened, and decanted it. He put the potatoes in the oven, the steak on the indoor grill, and pulled the lettuce out and cut it into a wedge. This was his nightly ritual.

Once in a rare moment of self-doubt he had talked to Terry Stevens, the head of one of the many alcohol support groups his firm represented.

"Terry," he had asked, "is there a test to determine whether a person who drinks regularly is an alcoholic?"

Terry replied, "An alcoholic can go days and weeks without a drink, but once he or she starts, they cannot stop until they are totally inebriated. That said, the best test is to drink two drinks a day, no more no less, for thirty days. If a person can do that, they are not an alcoholic. Could you do that?"

"I don't know, I've had more than that on a regular basis, and I don't get drunk. But I drink every day," Tommy replied.

Terry thought a minute and then said, "Alcohol has some control of your life, but you are quite functional in spite of that. I would say you are a functional alcoholic."

What Terry had told him bothered him because Tommy had to be in total control of his life and the circumstances which affected it; but since he was functional, he could live with it.

After dinner, Tommy cleaned his dishes and put them into the dishwasher. He poured the remainder of the bottle of wine into his glass and went back outside to stare into the lights. If Alex was right and whatever decision he was going to make over the weekend was in God's hands, he sure wished God would hurry up and help him decide. Otherwise, he would have to do it on his own.

CHAPTER EIGHT

The next morning Tommy went through his daily workout, showered, and changed. This being Saturday, it meant it was the day for his weekly visit with his mother, Luisa. He had been born the only child of Patrick Thomas O'Reilly and Luisa Maria (née Rizzo) O'Reilly and christened Thomas Patrick; he had the good fortune of receiving the best genes of his Irish father and his Italian mother.

His father, "Paddy," as he had been fondly called since childhood, was an outgoing sort, always ready for a good story followed by a hearty laugh. As a natural result of his bubbly personality and his genuine affection for Irish whiskey and Guinness stout (and not necessarily in that order), Paddy had owned an Irish pub. Paddy's, the only appropriate name for such an establishment, was located in the heart of downtown Houston.

The pub was a good business, and Paddy always generated enough income that Luisa and Tommy never wanted for anything within reason. The downside was that Paddy felt compelled to be at the pub from the time it opened until closing. It was open 363 days a year, the only abstentions being Christmas and Easter, as demanded by Luisa. That did not allow for much family time, and Tommy did not see much of his father during his childhood years. Luisa was determined that her only son would have all his needs met, so she took up the slack.

Paddy had been born and raised a Catholic, but he treated Catholicism like the other things he had been born with. He just accepted that he had red hair, blue eyes, and a large build, and also that he was a Catholic. There was nothing Paddy could do about any of them, and nothing about any of them to get excited about. Luisa, on the other hand, felt very deeply about her Italian heritage and Catholic religion, and she did her utmost to share her feelings with the two men in her life. Since Paddy was not around much, her efforts fell on Tommy. She made sure he attended the parochial school, daily Mass, was an altar boy, and followed all the rules.

In high school, Luisa had insisted that Tommy enroll in Bishop Brennan High School, the only co-educational Catholic high school in Houston. Upon graduation he was offered a full football scholarship to the University of Houston. Tommy was flattered, and Paddy was justifiably proud. Luisa was neither. She wanted more for Tommy. She wanted him to attend St. Thomas College, a small Catholic college in Houston. She wanted him to continue his all-important Catholic education in hopes that it would eventually lead to a religious vocation. For the first time in his life, Tommy did not follow his mother's wishes. It had been a defining moment because Tommy had not felt guilty.

After Paddy died, Luisa stayed by herself in the house in which they had lived those many years.

But age and arthritis had caught up with her, and Tommy found space in an assisted living center on the west part of town. It was run by the Sisters of Mercy, who helped convince Luisa that it was an appropriate option. In order to be ambulatory, Luisa needed a walker, and the care the attendants gave her was first class. A local priest said Mass daily and heard confessions often. Although Tommy would call her periodically during the week, Saturday was the one day he had alone with his mother, and he enjoyed the special time with his mom very much.

This particular Saturday, Tommy called down for his roadster, a Panoz 1997 AIV. There were less than three hundred of them made, and its all-aluminum body with a handmade aluminum Cobra engine made it the fastest production automobile ever made in the United States at the time. His roadster didn't have a top, and it was a great spring day when Tommy roared out of the Houston Towers headed to visit his mom.

When he arrived at the center, Luisa was waiting for him in the lobby.

"Hi, Mom," Tommy said as he kissed her on the cheek. "That dress you're wearing makes you look more beautiful than ever."

"Hello, Tommy," Luisa said as she hugged him back. "Wherever did you get such a gift of Irish blarney?"

They both smiled at each other while momentarily lost in thoughts of Paddy. Tommy broke the silence and said, "It's such a great day. Let's sit in the garden."

She whole-heartedly agreed, and they went out into the garden, Luisa in her walker, and Tommy walking slowly beside her.

After some talk about how each was health wise, during which Tommy seemed somewhat preoccupied, Luisa asked, "Is there something bothering you?"

"Oh, just the usual stuff at work. Why do you ask?" Tommy answered.

"I'm your mother. Or have you forgotten? You seem preoccupied. Is there anything you want to talk about?" Luisa replied.

"Well, there's something I have to get resolved in my own mind this weekend. A potential new client came to see me yesterday who wants to sue the Catholic Church. But it's not one of the sex scandal cases. This is entirely different," Tommy said.

Luisa looked at Tommy in a knowing way. "Okay. Again, do you want to talk about it?"

"Probably not, since I already know your thoughts." Tommy shrugged.

"Maybe not. I might surprise you," Luisa said with a smile.

Tommy took a deep breath and said, "Mom, she wants to be a priest. She believes that the laws against discrimination of women give her the right to require the Catholic Church to grant her admission to the seminary," Tommy finally said.

Luisa was silent for a long time. Finally she asked, "Do our laws give her that right? I find it hard to believe that they do."

"I don't know. Maybe they do. We're researching that question over the weekend, and I'll know more about that Monday morning."

Again there was silence, and then Luisa said, "Tommy, you've lived a charmed life. Things always came easy to you. When you had a rare setback, such as your knee injury in college that stopped your potential pro football career, the luck of the Irish led you to Joe Bob Finley after you had finished law school. Then when Mr. Finley had his untimely demise, you received a great fortune that became yours and yours alone. To your credit, you've used the money to do good things. But, Tommy, things have always come easy for you. You've never had to work for what you have achieved."

"But, Mom," Tommy interrupted.

"No, let me finish! You've never been confronted with a hard decision. As a matter of fact, you've avoided those decisions all of your life. Take women, for example. After a period of time when the relationship gets to a point where you would have to decide to make a commitment, you avoid the commitment and walk away."

This conversation was going the way he thought it would: *not well.* Tommy smiled and said, "Mom, maybe I haven't found the right person. Maybe my standards are too high. Maybe I'm trying to find someone just like the one who married dear old dad. Maybe there's not another one like you out there."

"Stop it, Tommy! This is what I'm talking about. You're avoiding a serious conversation with me and you're resorting to your cute little 'aw shucks' attitude that you use when you're uncomfortable. This is a big decision you are about to make, Tommy, perhaps the only one you have ever made. Have you really thought about what's involved here?" Luisa said determinedly.

"What do you mean?" Tommy asked.

"What do I mean? Have you considered what the Catholic Church is? Do you think it's a mean bunch of people? Do you think the Catholic Church hates women? Do you think the Catholic Church has no respect for women? The Virgin Mary, the mother of our Lord, is the most revered of all saints. If the Catholic Church has a rule against women serving as priests, do you think it's out of disrespect to women, or is it based upon a fundamental belief that such is in conformance with the wishes of God?" Luisa answered.

"No, I don't think the Catholic Church is mean-spirited but perhaps misdirected. I think the Catholic Church has a doctrine based upon the teachings of Jesus, but when men in the church begin to interpret those teachings, they can make mistakes," Tommy answered.

"But you don't know that's the case in this instance, do you?" Luisa responded.

Tommy shrugged his shoulders and said, "No, I don't. I don't know the basis upon which the church relies to exclude women from the priesthood. But discrimination of women in our country is not allowed unless there's a good reason to do so. For example, if the physical attributes of a woman would not allow her to withstand the physical rigors that a particular job required, it would be legal to exclude her from consideration solely because of her gender. I don't see that being the case here, but in any event, our judicial system will allow the church to explain its reasons for doing so if we get that far."

"You still don't get it, do you? Have you considered what you would be doing to me if you bring this lawsuit?" Luisa said, staring hard at Tommy.

"Okay, you're right. I don't get it! I don't know what you mean. What would I be doing to hurt you?" Tommy responded heatedly.

"Tommy, you're good at what you do, maybe one of the best. I assume you would not file a lawsuit unless you thought you had a chance, and a good chance, to succeed in a judgment for your client," Luisa responded with just as much anger.

Tommy nodded.

"They say that many times an innocent act has unintended negative consequences. Have you considered the unintended consequences to me and sixty million other Catholics in the United States? If you were to win your lawsuit, you'll drastically change our religion. You, as one person, will forever change our religion as we have known it all our lives. Do you really think you have a right to do this? And for what? Because some silly girl you've only known for a matter of hours has a crazy idea that she wants to be a priest?" Luisa was very angry now.

"If that happens, Mom, it will not be me that will cause the change. It will be the laws of the United States that will demand it. We are a nation of laws, and no one person and no institution, including the Catholic Church, should be above the law."

Exasperated, she shook her head and said, "You're doing it again, Tommy. You're avoiding the facts. If you decide to pursue this, you alone will be responsible for the consequences of your actions, nobody else. You and your laws will interfere with the rights of all Catholics to practice their religion as they wish. No government should ever have the right to tell anyone how they should worship. I thought that was a right we had in this country. Now you tell me we don't."

"No, Mother, I didn't tell you that! There is the right of religion guaranteed by the First Amendment to the Bill of Rights. Women also have the right to non-discrimination solely because of their gender. Which one rules in this case? I don't know, but as I told you, we're researching that question this weekend," Tommy said angrily.

"What about the laws of God, Tommy? All you are researching are the laws of men and their governments. Are you researching the laws of God? Where do the laws of God play in your decision?" she asked.

"I'm not sure they do." Tommy paused. "Well, maybe they do. If the basis of the church's discrimination of women is a biblical direction from Jesus, then that should be a valid reason to discriminate. I'll just have to find out the Catholic Church's reasoning and how they justify what they do. As you said, they are not mean people."

"Who's going to make that decision, Tommy? You?" Luisa asked.

"Yes."

"You and you alone will make this decision? What gives you the right to make this decision?" Luisa screamed.

They glared at each other for a moment, and then Luisa said quietly and with sadness and resignation in her voice, "If you decide to do this, Tommy, to sue the Catholic Church to force it to make a woman a priest, I don't know if I'll ever be able to forgive you. And I mean that Tommy. May God help you with this decision of *yours*." With that, she slowly got up out of her chair, positioned herself into her walker, and slowly retreated out of the garden into the main building without looking back and without another word.

Tommy watched her go inside, and after a while he got up to go himself. He walked through the lobby of the center, said good-bye to the receptionist, and walked to his roadster in the parking lot. He exited the parking lot and in minutes was on the freeway. Tommy was angry and hurt. He jammed the big gas pedal, and the little roadster immediately leaped forward. In an instant he was doing eighty miles an hour, and the wind began to buffet his face. He felt tears begin to form in his eyes, but since he wasn't wearing sunglasses, he couldn't be sure if they were the result of the wind or not.

CHAPTER NINE

That evening Tommy was in his apartment when the intercom rang. "Ms. Butler is here to see you, sir."

Tommy replied, "Thank you, George. Please send her up." Nikki Butler was, as the politically correct would say, Tommy's significant other. Tommy preferred to think of Nikki as his girlfriend.

They had met, oddly enough, in the courtroom. Seven months earlier, Tommy was representing Danny Horton, a seven-year-old second-grade student in one of the grade schools in a local school district. Both of Danny's parents were employed by a government contractor and were stationed in Iraq. While they were overseas, Danny lived with his maternal grandparents. Danny, in a show of love and duty to his parents, began to wear a wristband of red and blue with a white star in the middle. The school had advised Danny to discontinue the wearing of a wristband or he would be sent home. Danny refused to comply with the school's orders, and he was dismissed until such time as he could comply with the mandatory dress code. Danny's grandparents knew Betty Lincoln from church, and they and Bobby were able to gain an immediate interview with

Tommy. He immediately filed for an injunction in state district court to require the school to admit Danny to attend classes. Tommy won a temporary injunction, which allowed Danny to attend class pending the final determination of a permanent injunction. Since the county attorney had lost the first round, the school board decided to enlist the services of one of the premier law firms in Houston, and Nikki, as a senior litigator of that firm, had drawn the case.

Nikki had argued forcefully that a uniform dress code was crucial in the public school system to ensuring orderly conduct. If one deviation was made to that code of conduct, then school-aged children would be able to wear paraphernalia designating gang memberships, sexually provocative dress, and the like, all of which were prone to creating dissension within the classroom. While the school and school district sympathized with Danny and his love of his parents, any exception to that code could have detrimental consequences. Tommy had relied on the First Amendment and Danny's right to free speech, and though not entirely within the dress code of the school district, the wristband could not be considered provocative. Judge Van Horn had noticed that Danny was wearing Converse tennis shoes and asked whether they were within the dress code. When he was told they were, he suggested that perhaps red and blue stripes could be tastefully painted on the shoes which already had a white star in their logo. This was a decision readily accepted by all parties.

After the hearing, Nikki had approached Tommy and given him her card, on which she had written her personal phone number. She had said nothing, turned, and walked away, giving Tommy a view of what he could only describe at the time as an incredible backside. Since she was well within his "daughter rule," probably in her early forties, and since he had no other relationship at the time, he had indeed called her and made a date to meet her for dinner. From then on, Tommy and Nikki had grown quite close.

As Nikki walked in the front door, Tommy was once again astounded by her beauty. No matter how many times he saw Nikki, it was like seeing her for the first time. She was tall for a woman, about five feet eight inches, with silky long blonde hair and blue eyes. Not light blue eyes like Tommy's, but a deep blue, almost indigo. In fact, her blonde hair and Barbie-like figure were so perfect one would suspect she had enhanced both. Tommy knew for a fact that both features were real. She was beautiful, intelligent, and witty, and he was glad she had chosen him to spend time with. Tonight she had on a pair of black, slim-fitting designer jeans and a designer T-shirt that did little to hide her physical assets. Nikki leaned in and kissed him, and he responded in kind.

"That's nice," she murmured.

"Do you remember what happened the first time you said that?" he asked back.

"Why do you think that I keep saying that every time we meet?" She smiled.

He smiled back and asked, "Low flyer on the rocks?"

She answered with her standard, "But of course."

As she settled in on the cushy leather sofa, Tommy prepared her a generous amount of Famous Grouse scotch whiskey over ice in a large glass tumbler. He was already working on his first Black Bush.

"What's for dinner?" she asked.

"I thought we would have take-out tonight. I'm really not in the mood to cook." he answered.

She looked at him quizzically. "Since when is the great chef not interested in cooking?"

"Since tonight. Although this may be a new one for me, tonight I want to talk to you and get your advice about something," he said cryptically.

Tommy O'Reilly asking anyone for advice from anyone was as common as a lunar eclipse, and she became alarmed. "Is something wrong? This is Saturday. How did your visit with Luisa go? It's not Luisa, is it? Is something wrong with your mother? Is she okay?"

"Yes, she's fine physically, but she's not okay with me," Tommy answered.

"You and Luisa have a problem? That's unusual; you're very close. What is it?" Nikki asked.

"That's what I want to talk about and maybe get some advice," he answered.

He took their drinks and led her outside to the terrace on the north side where there was a cool breeze. Without speaking they both sat down in chairs side by side, allowing them both to take in the expansive view in front of them. It was another crisp and clear night, and the lights of the tall buildings of the medical center seemed close enough to touch. Beyond, the lights of the skyscrapers in downtown Houston seemed to melt into a flat carpet of light stretching north to the horizon. The blinking lights of the large airplanes lining up in the landing pattern for Houston Intercontinental Airport thirty miles away dotted the sky.

He looked at her and said, "Perhaps the best way to start is with Aleksandra Kowalski. She's a potential new client whom I talked to yesterday." He described his interview with Alex, the research assignments that he had given his lawyers and investigators to do over the weekend, and concluded with his volatile visit with Luisa that morning.

"Do you believe in God, Tommy?" she asked.

Tommy noticed both of their glasses were empty. Silently he stood up, taking her glass from her hand, and went into the bar and refilled them both. Returning to the terrace, he handed Nikki her glass and again sat down beside her.

"Are you avoiding my question? Do you believe in God?" she asked again.

"No, I'm not avoiding your question. It's a simple yes or no question, but to answer it fully, I need to give you an explanation so that you can understand why I answer the question the way I do."

"Go ahead, Tommy. We have all night," she said.

"For me," Tommy began, "all of the intangible aspects of my life such as trust, respect, and belief in someone or something must be learned. I don't take someone or something on face value. I'm guided by actions and facts. Once I get to know a person and watch what they say and do, then I can make a decision whether to trust or respect that person. I cannot believe in someone or something on faith alone. I have to have proof. As to your question about God, I was raised Catholic, and the core of Catholicism is the belief in God as a matter of faith. As I got older, I decided that if God existed, there had to be proof of that existence. I could believe if the facts proved an existence. If not, then I could not. As I began to research that question, it led me to science. Does science point to or go away from the existence of God? I asked myself."

He continued, "I examined the science of cosmology. Until the twentieth century, the universal belief of scientists was that the universe was eternal and static. The universe had always existed and would always exist. There was no proof of a beginning and therefore no expectations of an ending. Two things occurred that changed scientific thought. The first was Albert Einstein and his theory of relativity. The second was the Hubble telescope. Both proved that the universe was not static but in a continual state of expansion. The more distant the galaxies are in the universe, the faster the expansion. If something is expanding, then at some time in the past that something had to have been continually smaller and denser to the point at the beginning, which is nothing. Atheists believe this too but explain it away with the Big Bang, which was the sudden expansion of primordial elements. Unfortunately for them the laws of science state that something cannot arrive out of nothing. That is impossible. Whatever was there had to be created first, and whatever or whoever created it had to be beyond the bounds of scientific laws. Am I boring you?"

"Hardly." She shook her head. "Please go on."

"I looked at the laws of physics. There are thirty different fundamental principles of physics that have to be present to enable the existence of the universe, and they are all precisely balanced. Even if just one was slightly, and I mean slightly to a degree that is so small as to be out of the realm of comprehension, we, and all we know, could not exist. These parameters are so finely tuned that the possibility of this occurring by accident, and not design, is way beyond one in twenty to the hundredth power, which is a number that most mathematicians agree is infinitesimal and improbable. Science would say that the physical balance could not have been caused randomly. Therefore, the only logical conclusion is that it was accomplished through design. Einstein said it best when he said, 'I am convinced that God does not play dice.' A design obviously requires a designer.

"Should I go on?" he asked.

She nodded yes.

"The science of biochemistry tells us the human cell is very complicated, and there are fifty to a hundred trillion cells in a human body. Within a cell are extremely complex molecular machines. These machines have rotors, stators, and drive shafts that operate within a superb design. There are no mathematically possible odds of this design occurring randomly. This again suggests the required role of a designer. The DNA in the human cell is incredibly complex. DNA contains information, and where does information come from? Information cannot come from nonliving manner. The only known source for information is intelligence. So in summary, science leads me to the existence of a designer with intelligence," Tommy said as he finished.

Nikki thought for a moment and then said, "Okay, Tommy, science leads you to the conclusion of an intelligent design and designer. Many people believe that but also say that does not lead to God. They believe that the designer started the ball rolling, and the ball continues to roll without any further involvement of the designer. Is that where you are?"

Tommy immediately answered, "No. Whatever power and intelligence that created the universe has by definition to be beyond any constraints of time or space. Why would that power with such immense logic do something illogical? I know others disagree, but it isn't possible for me to conceive that such a super intelligence, with the evidence we can see everywhere through our own eyes and the eyes of science, could operate in an illogical manner. Where is the logic in creating the universe and leaving it alone?

"Throughout recorded time, man has been in awe of that which he could sense but not understand. Since man was afraid of those things, he worshiped them: the moon, the stars, the tides, and the weather, and many more. Man has worshiped many gods throughout time, and invariably many at the same time. There is only one religion that historically worshiped just one God, and that is the one found in Jewish scriptures. It's the only religion that had logical reasons for the design of creation. All other religions worshiped gods they could see, feel, or otherwise perceive with their senses but could not understand. The Hebrews had a God they could not see, feel, or otherwise perceive with their senses, but they believed operated in a logical manner. The facts tell me that there is an intelligent designer, one who by definition has to operate logically, and the designer and creator found in Jewish scripture is the only one which does that."

"So your answer is you do believe in the God of the Jewish religion?" Nikki asked.

"Yes, I do, for the reasons I have stated." Tommy answered.

"Are you a Christian?" asked Nikki.

"This again requires an explanation," he answered.

"You're complicated," she said, laughing.

He smiled and said, "Remember, you asked for it. In order to be a Christian, a person has to believe that Jesus of Nazareth lived, died, and rose from the dead. There are an abundant number of historical resources that prove that Jesus of Nazareth lived at the time the Christian Scriptures say he did. The Romans were intense about recording their activities, and there are a number of Roman texts that reference Jesus of Nazareth. There are a number of Jewish historical references that do as well. Historical evidence states that Jesus of Nazareth did exist. Jewish scriptures also frequently talk about a Messiah to come. Was Jesus of Nazareth the Messiah described in those texts? Again, the answer is yes, and it is conclusive."

"Is it really?"

"Most definitely."

Tommy continued, "A number of prophecies in their Scriptures were very specific about who the Messiah would be. He would be born in the tribe of Judah, the family of Jesse, in the house of David. He would be betrayed by a friend for thirty pieces of silver, and he would be crucified, even though crucifixion was *unknown* at the time of the prophecies. The prophecies also foretold that King Herod would sentence all Jewish males two years and under to death, and the Messiah and his family would flee to Egypt. There are many more, the last prophecy being four hundred years before the birth of Jesus of Nazareth."

He paused, took a sip of his Black Bush, then continued, "Some mathematicians took just eight of the prophecies and calculated the odds of one person fulfilling those specific prophecies. The odds are one out of ten to the seventeenth power. While within the realm of possibility, if one were to take silver dollars equal to that number and lay them across the state of Texas, it would result in a layer of silver dollars two feet deep. Let's assume one were to mark just one of those dollars and bury it somewhere in the two-feet-deep pile of silver dollars across Texas. Let's assume we blindfold a man and have him walk across Texas and with just one choice try to pick the one silver dollar that was marked. The odds of doing that would be equal to the odds of one man fulfilling those eight prophecies. Then the same mathematicians took the total forty-eight prophecies that matched the life of Jesus of Nazareth, and determined the odds of that occurring are one in twenty to the one hundred and fifty-seventh power. As we know, the odds of anything over one in twenty to the hundredth power are infinitely improbable."

"So you believe Jesus lived and is the Messiah described in Jewish scriptures?" Nikki asked.

"Yes," Tommy answered.

"Does that make him the Son of God, who is the core of Christianity?" Nikki asked.

"That depends if he did something that no person has ever done or could ever do: rise from the dead. We know for certain from the historical documents I mentioned earlier he was crucified. Did the crucifixion lead to his death or had he fainted on the cross? Crucifixion was a Roman staple. The centurion in charge of any crucifixion was bound to ensure the death of the crucified before taking him down from the cross. Failure to do so would cause the centurion to lose his life. Therefore, the centurion took the matter quite seriously. The normal method of ensuring death was to break the bones of the prisoner. Even if the prisoner was unconscious, he would react to that. While the two victims on either side of Jesus had their bones broken, Jesus did not. Instead, this particular Centurion stabbed a spear into his side, which historians believe was into his heart, ensuring his death. This set of events was incidentally prophesied in the Jewish Scriptures and, again, before crucifixion was known. So I believe the evidence would indicate beyond a reasonable doubt that Jesus was dead."

Tommy's face became more animated as he continued. "Now, the real question is, did he come back from that death? We have eyewitness testimony of more than five hundred people who saw Jesus after his death. He appeared alive to them in thirteen separate instances. Were they lying? Why would they? It was not for money that they would've said this. There is no rational reason for them to have said what they did except that it was the truth. In fact, by doing so, all of them were ostracized in the society in which they lived. Most of them died horrible deaths through torture when they could have avoided that by renouncing Jesus as the Messiah. Yet none of them did. They knew what they had seen and convinced thousands and thousands of others of that fact. You are a lawyer, Nikki. What do you think the odds are of winning a case with five hundred eyewitnesses and not one witness who can say otherwise? That is powerful evidence. So in summary, Nikki, I believe the facts bear out that Jesus of Nazareth lived, that he was the Messiah prophesied in the Jewish Scriptures, and that he died and arose from that death. I believe he is the Son of God."

Nikki looked at Tommy for a while and said, "So in summary, you have proven to yourself that you believe in God and are a Christian. Is that right?"

"Yes."

"There are thousands of Christian faiths in existence today," Nikki began, "so why are you a Catholic Christian?"

Tommy answered, "History tells us that it was the first and original church. If I can have the original of anything, why would I settle for a copy?"

Nikki thought a moment. "Do you pray?"

"Never, Nikki. Why would I?"

CHAPTER TEN

Tommy noticed that their glasses were empty. "Do you want to order some take-out, or do you want another drink?" Tommy asked Nikki.

"If it's all the same to you, I'll take another drink. I'm really not hungry right now, and I like the conversation we're having. In the seven months I've known you, this is the first time you've opened up to me like you're doing tonight," Nikki answered.

"That's fine with me, Nikki. If we get hungry later, I'll make us a BLT." He took her glass and with his own left the balcony and went back into the bar. He returned with the two drinks and one of his Cusano eighteen-year-old cigars. He handed her the drink, lit his cigar, and leaned back in his chair. Nikki had many fine attributes, but one of her better ones was that she enjoyed the smell of a good cigar.

"It's your turn now, Nikki. What do you believe?" Tommy asked.

"I believe in God, because like you, it doesn't make sense to me not to. However, I've never been involved with an organized religion. My parents were part of the hippie subculture and were flower children. They were actually at Woodstock. They were very sweet and loving to me and my younger brother. We both had great childhoods. They did not believe in showing a child the path to take, but tried to prepare their children for whatever paths they would take. So when it came to organized religion, they encouraged the lessons of the Bible but allowed us to choose the religion that best fulfilled our own beliefs. So far I haven't found one, but I admit I haven't been looking very hard. I'm not sure one needs an organization to have a meaningful relationship with God."

She continued, "But from what you have said, Tommy, I assume you disagree with that. You've chosen an organized religion, Catholicism. Do you believe everything the Catholic Church teaches?"

"Of course not," Tommy responded firmly. "The Catholic Church has been wrong many times. I believe in the core doctrine of the Catholic Church, which is based upon the teachings of Jesus as provided in the Scriptures. Where the church makes mistakes is when it tries to interpret those teachings and gets into the man-made rules. It has happened many times in the past, and who's to say everything the church says today will be what it says tomorrow?"

"If, as you say, they have changed direction many times, I assume you can give me at least one example," Nikki said.

"But of course." Tommy smiled, using one of her favorite responses. "Let's take for an example the church's teaching on the celibacy of the clergy. Celibacy was not taught by Christ. As far as we know, many of the apostles were married and had children. In the early church years, we know that many priests, bishops, and even popes were married. There were several instances of lineal heirs to popes being ordained a pope. Although there was only one occasion of the son of a pope being named pope upon his father's death, grandchildren and great-grandchildren of popes being named pope was not abnormal. Centuries later, a change was made that prohibited a priest from marrying *only after* ordination. Then in the seventeenth century, the rule of celibacy as it is taught today was enacted, and more importantly, enforced. Many historians believe the rule was enacted not out of a desire to dissuade a cleric from temporal desires, but to avoid the practical effect of feudal laws. Feudal law required the firstborn son to inherit the estates of the father, and this would put the title to church land on which the priest/ father lived in dispute after his death. The ban of marriage for a cleric relegated any such offspring of a cleric to be illegitimate, with no legal standing to inherit the estate of his father/priest, a rather tidy solution to what could have been a difficult legal problem."

She pondered what he said for a minute and took a sip of her scotch. "Okay, now let's get to the real issue about what you and Luisa discussed, and, I assume, what you wanted to talk to me about. Let's talk about the rule of male-only priests. What is the church's reasoning behind that?" Nikki asked. "Is that one of the man-made rules you talk about, or is it based upon the teaching of Jesus?"

"I don't know. I have to assume that the church has a solid foundation from the Scriptures for the rule. I'll have to find out what it is and see if it makes sense," Tommy replied.

Nikki asked, "I believe you said you owe your client an answer by Monday. Are you going to determine the reasoning of the Catholic Church behind a male-only clergy in the next twenty-four hours?"

"Yes, I hope to do so," Tommy responded.

"You just said you would have to find out if it makes sense. Does that mean you alone will decide whether it is sensible?" Nikki asked dubiously.

"Yes," Tommy said.

"You intend to do that with no guidance from anybody else?" Nikki asked.

"That's correct. As we talked about earlier tonight, I will do my own research, and if it makes sense to me, then I can believe it. If it doesn't make sense to me, then I can't. I don't have to rely upon anybody else to decide it for me," Tommy answered.

"Upon what basis would you make that decision?" Nikki inquired.

"As I've told you, Nikki, I don't take things on faith, but I base my decisions on facts. Hopefully the basis will be a direct quotation from the Scriptures specifically requiring a priest to be a male. But it might be something else. I don't know. I'll have to see," Tommy said.

There were several minutes of total solitude, each staring into the night with their own thoughts and drinks. Finally Nikki broke the silence and turned to Tommy and said, "Oh, Tommy, I'm so afraid for you. You know I'm attracted to you, maybe a lot, but even if I were attracted to you just a little, I would still be afraid. What you're telling me is this: depending upon the legal research being done as we speak, and assuming that the research is positive about your ability to legally obtain jurisdiction over the Catholic Church in US federal court, whether or not you file suit will depend upon whether you believe the Catholic Church has a logical reason requiring priests to be males. Is that what you're telling me?" Nikki asked pointedly.

"Yes, I haven't thought about it in those exact terms, but yes, that's what I'm saying," Tommy answered.

"That's why I'm afraid for you. You're about to make a decision that could affect millions of lives based solely upon your determination of whether the church is right or wrong. Tommy, you're playing God," she said, looking at him sadly.

Tommy shook his head and started to interrupt.

"No, Tommy, let me please finish. That's exactly what you are doing. Apparently this has been a teaching of the Catholic Church for two thousand years. During that time there have been tens of thousands, if not hundreds of thousands, of dedicated clerics who have devoted their lives to fulfilling God's word on this earth. Even you would have to recognize that decisions made by these dedicated people would not be made lightly. And these people, whether you or others believe it or not, believe they are the representatives of God here on earth. What they collectively decide they believe is the will of God. They must believe that what they say to be the appropriate gender of a priest *is* the will of God. How can you, one person, in twenty-four hours decide what they say is or is not the will of God? Because you say it will either make sense to you or not? Tommy, you're playing God. And that's why I'm afraid for you." She turned and stared into the night, not wanting to look at him.

"Nikki, this isn't about playing God. This is about a woman who has rights under the law, and the Catholic Church or any other institution or person in this country cannot violate those rights without good reason. Once I know the reason, I will know whether it fits the legal definition of 'good reason.' That's my job, Nikki. I'm a lawyer. Nothing more, nothing less," Tommy said heatedly.

She turned to him and said just as heatedly, "The legal definition of 'good reason,' or Tommy O'Reilly's definition of 'good reason'? Yes, you are lawyer, but you're also a person, and I thought until tonight a good person. But you're showing me tonight something about you I haven't seen before. You're arrogant to think that whatever makes sense to you is right, no matter how many other people with better qualifications than you think it's wrong. That's scary, Tommy, and it makes me scared and afraid for you."

With that, she got up and started heading for the door. "I'm not going to stay the night, Tommy. I'm going home. Don't bother to get up. I know my way out. You need all the time alone to think about what you're going to do. Although you say you never pray, you might want to think that one over again. I believe you will need all of the support of the god you say you believe in you can get."

With that Nikki left and quietly shut the front door. Tommy was alone with his thoughts, drink, and cigar. As he drew on his cigar, he could not escape the feeling, the very uncomfortable feeling, that in one day he had greatly disappointed the two most important women in his life. And try as he might to think of positive outcomes in what lay ahead, a sense of foreboding kept clawing its way back.

CHAPTER ELEVEN

Tommy awoke Sunday morning and dispensed with his usual workout routine. He pulled on a light pair of casual khaki slacks, a dark green short-sleeved polo, and a light beige sleeveless sweater. Last, he pulled on a well-worn pair of peanut-butter-colored ostrich skin boots. He drove to Our Lady of Faith Catholic Church. After seven thirty a.m. Mass, he waited until he was the last to leave the front entrance of the church. As he knew it would be, Father Damien was at the door greeting parishioners as they left.

"Hello, Tommy," Father Damien greeted him warmly. "How have you been? I don't believe I've seen you in a while."

"Hello, Father, I must be attending the masses you don't officiate," Tommy replied.

"That's what your father used to tell me as well." Father Damien frowned. "I didn't believe him either."

Tommy reddened and mumbled, "Sorry, Father, I was just … Well, never mind." Then in a louder voice, Tommy said, "I hope you have some spare time to talk to me, Father. I can meet with you anytime today, but I would like to do it now, if it's convenient."

R.A. BROWN

"I'm Pastor Emeritus now Tommy, which means I only have one Mass on Sunday, and that's the one you just attended. I have the time now, if you'd like."

Tommy nodded his head, and Father Damien said, "Let me get these vestments off, and I will meet you in the garden."

Father Damien had been at Our Lady of Faith parish since Tommy was ten years old. Father Damien had been newly ordained when he first came to Our Lady of Faith, so Tommy guessed he was fifteen-plus years older than Tommy, so he would be in his seventies now. He had always been a slight spry man, and he still had that same bounce in his step. His dark hair had given way to gray and had become thinner. Other than the wrinkles that age imposes, he still looked the same.

Tommy entered the garden, which was about the size of three of the classrooms in the school which it abutted. It was also next to the rectory and church. It was oftentimes used for cake sales, raffle ticket sales, and other types of endeavors that the parish guilds would use to raise money for the church. Today it was empty, and Tommy was thankful for that. Father Damien walked into the garden in a black cassock that seemed to be the norm for a parish priest. They sat down on park benches at the side of the garden near enormous red rose bushes, which were starting to bloom. They were across from each other, and Father took out a packet of Marlboro Red cigarettes from the pocket of his cassock. As long as Tommy could remember, Father Paul Damien had smoked Marlboro Reds. He shook one out of the packet, put it to his lips, lit it, inhaled deeply with his mouth open in a half yawn, then exhaled the smoke through pursed lips. *Father Damien does enjoy his cigarettes,* Tommy thought.

"I thought the church frowned on priests smoking in front of parishioners," Tommy joked.

"What makes you think you're a parishioner?" Father Damien laughed. "Parishioners attend Mass regularly."

"You make a valid point." Tommy laughed back. "How do you like the Pastor Emeritus gig?" Tommy asked.

"It's a pretty good deal. Since us old folks tend to get up early, I get the early Mass every Sunday. That allows the younger priests to sleep in, which they like. Plus they get the larger congregations at the later masses to hear the words of wisdom in their homilies. Most of the older parishioners like the seven thirty Mass, so I might get to see old friends, such as you today. I don't know if most of the celebrants are here because they're old like me and get up early, or they know I say the Mass, and it seems like old times."

"I'm sure it's the latter, Father Damien. You're a fixture around here," Tommy said sincerely.

"You didn't come here to talk about my status. What do you have on your mind, Tommy?"

"I want to know what the qualifications are for the priesthood," Tommy replied.

"We're not thinking about a career change, now, are we?" Father Damien chuckled. "You might meet the basic qualifications, but I suspect you may have a problem with the procedures that follow."

"You know me better than that, Father. But I would like to discuss the qualifications and the procedures that you mentioned."

Puzzled, Father Damien asked, "May I know the reason for your curiosity?"

"To the extent I can under attorney-client privilege, I will tell you what I'm working on, but I would like to save it until the end. Consider that I have a hypothetical candidate for the priesthood."

"That's fair enough," Father Damien answered. "The qualifications are very basic. To be a candidate for priesthood one has to be an unmarried male baptized in the Catholic religion."

"That's it?"

"That's it," Father Damien replied and then continued, "I told you that you would meet the basic qualifications. Now comes the hard part, the procedures that attempt to satisfy the intangible qualifications."

After a moment of reflection he asked, "Does your hypothetical candidate want to be a member of an order, or a diocesan priest?"

"Does it matter? Are the procedures different?" Tommy asked.

"They are very much so. The procedures for the Jesuit order would be different from those of the Franciscan order. In turn, the procedures for a diocese may be different from those of the orders, and again will vary from diocese to diocese. If it helps your hypothetical candidate any, I am the most familiar with the procedures in the Archdiocese of Galveston-Houston. Should I proceed on that basis?" Father Damien asked.

Tommy nodded yes, and Father Damien stubbed out his cigarette on the ground and put the butt into a pocket of his cassock. From the other pocket he took out his cigarettes, lit one, and began to speak. "The first step in the procedure involves the priests in the parish where the candidate resides. He will talk to one of the priests about his desire for a vocation, and the ball starts rolling from there. He will talk to other priests in the parish, and based upon what they know about him, including his spirituality, personality, and dedication toward the priesthood, they may or may not recommend him to the diocese. Only if the priests in the parish in which he lives recommend him for admittance to the seminary will the application of the candidate be considered by the vocation office in the archdiocese. At that point a number of interviews are arranged with the candidate with different people. The purpose of these interviews is to determine whether the candidate possesses the intangible qualities required for the priesthood. Among these qualities are: a love for the Catholic faith, generosity, a desire to help other people, a personal relationship with God, a capacity and desire to learn, a healthy self-image, good social skills, and the ability to enjoy one's own company since the priesthood is a solitary life. With the advent of the priest scandals in the church, a new element has been added to the screening process, and that is an interview with one or more psychologists or psychiatrists. The purpose of the interviews is to gather objective data about the personality characteristics of the candidate."

Tommy made a mental note of the psychological interview. "What happens with the results of the interviews and tests? Are they compiled in written form?"

"Oh, yes. The church is very demanding of written documentation. The written documentation is submitted to the head of the diocese be he a bishop or archbishop. In the event that an application has been made to an order, then the submittal is to the head of the order. The ultimate decision whether to accept the candidate to the seminary lies with the head of the order or the bishop as the case may be. There is no appeal," Father Damien concluded.

"Okay, Father, now we come to the question that I came here to ask you. All of what you've told me has been very helpful, and I thank you very much for your insight. But let's assume my hypothetical candidate can pass all of the interviews with flying colors. Let's assume, further, that this candidate is outstanding in every respect but one, and that one is the lack of a penis," Tommy asked directly.

Father Damien sat back and stared Tommy in the eyes. There was a long moment of silence, and this man Tommy had known for years had a look on his face he knew he had never seen before. "Tommy, what do you mean? Are you out of your mind? You really can't mean this! It's ... It's ... I really don't know what to say."

CHAPTER TWELVE

Tommy put his elbows on his knees and leaned forward. Father Damien was avoiding his gaze and kept looking down at the ground. "Father Damien, please look at me, please."

The priest responded and raised his head and met Tommy's gaze.

Tommy began quietly but with earnest, "I know the Catholic Church will have a valid reason for excluding women from the priesthood. It's an institution that has dedicated two thousand years to doing God's work on this earth. I just want to know what those reasons are. Father Damien, I have known you most of my life. You've earned my trust and respect, and what you say to me will be very important. Would you please help me?"

Father Damien turned to stare at the rose bushes and lit another cigarette. He turned to face Tommy and said "Okay, Tommy, here it is. The most important reason is in 2005, Pope John Paul II stated as a matter of faith and morals that the priesthood was reserved to men only. When a pope speaks on issues of faith and morals, the church believes his word on that issue is infallible. That should be enough of a reason. End of discussion!"

"But, Father," Tommy pleaded, "the church had the same rule for almost two thousand years before 2005. What was the basis for the rule before John Paul issued his edict, and upon what did he base his decision? For example, are there any quotations from the Scriptures that require a male priesthood?"

"No, there are not. Less than twenty years ago a council of bishops met, researched, and reviewed that very question. Their conclusion is that there are no direct teachings in the Scriptures on this particular point," Father Damien answered.

"Father, if there is no direct teaching from the Scriptures, what could possibly be the basis?" Tommy asked.

"The fundamental basis is Jesus Christ did not name a woman to be one of his original apostles. The apostles were the first priests of the Catholic Church." Father Damien took another pull from his cigarette, exhaled, and said, "Jesus Christ was the son of God and came to earth to redeem us. He was very different from other males of that time, in that he treated women as equals. When he named the apostles, he could have chosen a woman if he so wished. At the time, many pagan religions had priestesses. To name a woman as an apostle would not have been out of the ordinary. He had many candidates such as his own mother, Mary, and Mary Magdalene, but he chose not to do so. When the eleven apostles chose the replacement for Judas they chose a man, not a woman. They knew the intent of Jesus as well as anyone. As the apostles began to ordain priests, there is no record of the ordination of a woman. Also, a priest is Christ's representative on earth. Christ was a man, not a woman, and as God he could have chosen to be a woman. He did not."

"So, Father, in absence of a scriptural direction or teaching, the church in essence bases its reasoning on something that Christ did not do but could have done?" Tommy asked.

"Yes."

"That's it?" Tommy asked incredulously.

"Pretty much. You can check me out if you want."

"Oh I will," Tommy said.

Tommy sat for a moment watching Father Damien smoke and then asked, "What about the other things Christ did not do and could have done that the church allows in the ordination of priests?"

Father Damien took on a puzzled look. "Can you give me an example?" he asked.

"Sure," Tommy said. "The twelve apostles were all Jewish, were they not?"

Father Damien nodded his head.

Tommy continued, "There were Gentiles among the followers of Jesus, and he could have easily named a Gentile as an apostle. Does the fact that he didn't mean all priests today should be Jewish?"

"That may have been more of a practical matter," Father Damien answered, "more to do with the customs of the times than an intention to bar Gentiles forever from the priesthood."

"The same can also be said about women," Tommy said bluntly.

Father Damien looked at Tommy but said nothing.

After several moments of silence, Tommy asked, "What about homosexuals? To our knowledge, none of the apostles were homosexual. In fact, to our knowledge, they were all married with children. If I remember correctly, the only early apostle who wasn't married was Paul. If Christ did not ordain a homosexual, why are they not barred from the priesthood today?"

Father Damien shifted on the bench in an uncomfortable way. Tommy thought he may have gotten into something that was personal to Father Damien. Father replied, "The church historically has not considered sexual orientation as a prerequisite of priesthood. However, with the recent scandals there has been some discussion that a homosexual is more likely to be a pedophile than a heterosexual, while there is no proof to that being true. There has been some direction from Rome to not accept known homosexuals to the seminary. However, the directions seem vague, and Rome has clarified that it is the ultimate decision of the bishops or the head of the order. I personally believe that regardless of sexual orientation, as long as a priest maintains his vow of celibacy, then his orientation should not make a difference. I have known homosexual priests, and they have been and are now excellent priests within every meaning of the word." Father Damien said this with such finality that Tommy felt he could be talking about a personal issue.

Tommy could not care less. "Jesus did not name Gentiles as priests, and all priests today are Gentiles. Jesus did not name women or homosexuals as priests, but the church today allows one and not the other, and they both have to do with sexual makeup. Does any of this make sense to you, Father?" Tommy inquired.

"It doesn't matter whether it makes sense to me or not, Tommy. The church is not a democracy. If someone doesn't like the rules, his only choice is to accept the rules or get out," Father Damien said.

"But this decision that affects the lives of hundreds of millions of women has been made by one man, Father, one man only, and that is the Pope. Are you okay with that?" Tommy asked.

"Before I answer that, I would like to clarify something. Based upon our discussion today, Tommy, I'm under the impression your hypothetical candidate is a woman client of yours who wants to be a priest," Father Damien said. "Could that possibly be correct?"

"Yes," Tommy answered.

"Following the outline of your questions, are you trying to make sense of the church's position and the reasons for the position?" Father Damien asked.

"Yes."

"And if the position or reasons of the church do or don't make sense to you, that will determine what you will do with your client?" Father Damien asked.

"Yes, Father, that's part of the equation."

"Then I will repeat the question you asked me. A decision is made by one man, and one man only, which affects the lives of hundreds of millions of people. Am I okay with that? On matters of faith and morals in the Catholic Church, I'm okay with the pope making that decision. I'm not okay with you making that decision, Tommy. I'm not okay with that at all."

With that, Father Damien got up, smoothed his cassock, and walked slowly to the rectory without shaking hands or saying goodbye. It did not escape Tommy's attention that this had been happening a lot to him lately.

CHAPTER THIRTEEN

Tommy walked into the office on Monday morning. As always, Betty was there to greet him.

"Good morning, boss. Scuttlebutt around here has it that you're out to get us all struck by lightning," Betty drawled.

Tommy glared at Betty and thought, *One of these days*, but he knew that would never happen.

Tommy replied dryly "Betty, if what you say happened, I would be truly *shocked.*"

Betty groaned and said, "*Comedy Central* is not in your future, boss. Better keep your day job. I have the conference room set up with coffee and kolaches, and Willis is in there now with Billie, Rickie, and Mr. Prentice discussing the results of their research over the weekend."

"Kolaches may keep you on the payroll, Betty. I would ask if the coffee is fresh, but I already know how you feel about coffee as part of your job description," Tommy said with resignation.

Tommy walked into the conference room, set down his briefcase, and poured a cup of coffee. He then chose a kolache stuffed with jalapeno Polish sausage and sat down at the conference table in the midst of a heated discussion. The discussion turned into murmurs and then silence, and then all faces turned toward Tommy.

"Silk, do you want to bring me up to date?" Tommy asked. "When I walked in it sounded like there might be some differences of opinion on something."

Willis said, "Let's start with Tim. His research is pretty straightforward."

Tim Prentice started reading from his notes. "Tommy, we did the most due diligence on Aleksandra Kowalski we could in the forty-eight hours you allowed us. We got a number of personal interviews with people outside her family and friends, including some former teachers, classmates, even a Girl Scout leader and a parish priest. We told them the purpose of the interview was for a potential job position. I didn't think that would be a question that would skew the answers. Suffice it to say, Alex has been an individual with the highest standards of integrity, leadership, and interpersonal skills of anyone that the interviewees had known. When I read the reports, I thought we'd been asking about Mother Teresa. We can keep looking, Tommy, but we had a large number in a broad spectrum of subjects we talked to."

"How many did you interview?" Tommy asked.

"Thirty-two," Tim answered.

"Keep looking. I don't want any surprises if we decide to proceed. What about your techno-nerds? Any surprises in the computer?"

Still reading from his notes, Tim said, "Nothing, absolutely nothing. She exists, but it's like she didn't exist. No traffic citations, no Facebook or Twitter pages, no references on those or any other web sites. Everybody has something on the Web, but not this girl. Don't get me wrong, her social security number checks, her addresses check, birth date, parents, everything checks. This is the vanilla girl."

"Instead of the vanilla girl, maybe she's the snow girl, as in pure as the driven," Tommy replied.

"So far that's what it seems like. But we'll keep looking," Tim said.

"Tim, I emphasize that the church has enormous resources, and they'll put them all to use to discredit Alex if we file the lawsuit. We have to know if there's anything out there that would discredit her qualifications for the priesthood other than her gender, anything at all."

"Got it, Tommy. We'll do our best."

"That's all I ask. All right, Silk, where are we on a legal basis for a lawsuit?"

Willis answered, "First of all, if we file this action, it will be a case of first impression. Our research shows that at no time, nowhere has this cause of action been raised in any state or federal court. A state court would've been a reach because of the federal questions involved, but we checked anyway. Does a US District Court have jurisdiction over the Catholic Church? The answer is yes, the church has been sued a number of times in the sex scandal cases, but never on an issue of ecclesiastical rules. But we have jurisdiction."

"So where does that leave us on the legal rights of the parties?" Tommy asked.

"In support of Ms. Kowalski, we have the Civil Rights Act of 1964 and its subsequent amendments, which prohibit the discrimination of women for employment without good cause," Willis responded and then continued. "The Civil Rights Act included a specific exclusion for employees of a church so that a church may legally discriminate against a potential employee because of gender. We don't think that exclusion applies in this instance. Our research indicates that a priest does not fit within the legal definition of an employee. At best, the priest would be an independent contractor. We believe it's irrelevant in any event, since we would be seeking an injunction to prohibit the archdiocese from excluding Ms. Kowalski from the seminary to study to become a priest because of her sex. A seminarian does not receive income in any way, shape, or form, so therefore cannot be an employee. The seminarian is a student. It's only after ordination that a priest could arguably be an employee by taking a position within a diocese or order.

"If Ms. Kowalski were to win the lawsuit, go to the seminary, and become ordained, we could take that fight up at that time. She could also set up her own parish without the support of a diocese or order and not be employed by anybody. We also have case law expanding the rights of women beyond areas of employment such as admission to venues that had been previously restricted to males, such as educational institutions, which a seminary certainly is. But never, and I repeat never, with reference to a church. On the flipside for the Catholic Church, there is the very definite First Amendment right to the separation of church and state, which prevents federal law from interfering with the operations of any church."

"When I came in," Tommy said, "there seemed to be a difference of opinion among the group about something. Can you enlighten me?"

Willis again replied, "There's a difference of opinion about whether we can get past a motion for summary judgment. We believe the defendant will file this motion immediately and ask the court to assume all the facts we have pled are valid, but as a matter of law, the court has no jurisdiction over the issue and will dismiss the lawsuit. We all agree that this is a very gray area. Alex may not have standing to sue as a matter of law because of the First Amendment requiring a separation of church and state, which results in the guarantee of freedom of religion. The judge could well rule against Alex on this issue. We all believe that it will depend upon the judge we draw."

Tommy took a sip of his coffee and then looked at Tim Prentice and asked, "Do you know who the most important person is in the United States?"

Tim looked puzzled and then answered, "The president, but what does he have do with this?"

"It's not the president, Tim. It's a federal district court judge, and from what I have heard so far, it sounds like he has everything to do with this," Tommy answered. "Unlike a president or a member of Congress, a federal district court judge is appointed for life, the only exception being impeachment due to the commission of a serious offense, which rarely happens. The president has to appease the voters and Congress to get anything done, and Congress has to appease the voters and the president to do their part. A federal district court judge has none of these checks and balances. The only oversights to a federal district court judge are the judges in the federal court of appeals, who are likewise federal judges appointed for life. Billie, you do a lot of appellate work. Please explain to Tim the likelihood of overturning a district court judge on appeal."

Billie looked at Tim and said, "The percentage of cases that are overruled by the appellate court is less than ten percent depending upon the jurisdiction. The only other appeal after that court's decision is to the US Supreme Court, which has the prerogative to decide whether to *even* hear the appeal or not. The number of times they decide to hear an appeal is miniscule compared to the number of cases filed. Of the many thousands of cases submitted to the Supreme Court each year, the court routinely hears less than a hundred."

Willis then chimed in, "The net result of what Tommy and Billie have said is that the judge in a United States federal court is the king. What he decides to be the truth based upon the testimony is rarely, if ever, overturned, and while his rulings of law are more likely to be reversed than his findings on the facts, if they are based upon sound legal reasoning, they likewise will be upheld. If a federal judge is so inclined, he can have a greater direct effect on the law in one year by himself than a congressman can directly effect by himself in a lifetime."

"I had no idea," Tim said. "Willis, you said whether we get thrown out will depend upon the judge we draw. What do you mean by that?"

"Most of us in the firm feel that federal judges fall into two broad categories. The first category is the conservative judge most often appointed by a Republican president and confirmed by the Senate. These judges tend to be strict constructionists and rely on the law as it presently stands. They feel that the enactment of laws is the role of the legislature, and their role is to interpret that law. The second category is the progressive judge, who is most likely to be appointed by a Democratic president and also approved by the Senate. This type of judge believes that the law is a growing body that has to be viewed with regard to an ever-changing society."

"Which kind do we have here in Houston?" Tim asked.

"Both kinds," Tommy answered.

"Which kind would be better for us?" Tim responded.

"The second kind," Tommy answered. "This would be a case never filed before. In a case of first impression, a judge in the first category would be reluctant to step outside of previous decisions, whereas a judge in the second category would be more inclined to adjust or expand existing law to a new set of facts."

"So how do we get the progressive judge?" Tim asked.

'We don't,' Willis responded. "When a complaint is filed in US District Court, the judge to be assigned to the case is randomly drawn. Whatever judge is drawn, that would be the judge the parties to the lawsuit would be stuck with for the duration of the case."

Tommy finished, "In summary, the odds of getting past a Motion for Summary Judgment will vary from slim and none with a conservative judge to maybe fifty-fifty with a progressive judge. It all depends upon the judge we draw."

Everyone but Tommy had the same thought, *Not very good odds.* Tommy thought, *Joe Bob would take fifty-fifty any time.*

"Okay, Tommy, let's assume we can get to the jury. What's our story?" Willis asked. As Joe Bob had taught Tommy and Tommy had taught Silk the real issue in a trial was not the facts of the case but "the story." By the time the case went to trial, the facts were pretty much established. The winning party was the one who had the best story and the best storyteller as a lawyer. While there may be a "he said, she said" element within the facts, the best storyteller could convey who was most likely telling the truth within the confines of the story. It was the best story that convinced the jury, the one that made the most sense in light of the facts. Tommy was very good at this, and Silk was not far behind. He had asked the right question.

"The fact that the Catholic Church discriminates against women by barring them from the priesthood solely because of their gender is a given," Tommy answered. "This discrimination is legal provided they have good reason to do so. I will relate to you what I've found out and what the church will most likely rely upon in this regard." Tommy then told them about his conversation with Father Damien and his subsequent research on church teachings on the Web the previous day.

Tommy continued, "There is universal agreement that there is no biblical reference for denying women the priesthood. The fact that Jesus could have included a woman as one of his apostles but did not do so seems to be the crux of the Catholic Church's argument. Jewish women in the time of Jesus were treated little better than slaves. One could argue then that was normal behavior of the time, and he might not have selected a woman apostle because of social norms. The church will counter that Jesus had treated women equally, much more so than anyone would or could expect at the time. Given his even treatment of women, the lack of a woman apostle is even more persuasive. Also, a number of pagan religions at the time had priestesses, so a woman apostle would have had a foundation for acceptance."

"That's a pretty good story and actually makes a lot of sense," Willis said. "What's yours?"

"I disagree, Silk. I don't think it makes much sense at all. Jesus was fulfilling the Jewish Scriptures and was working within the Hebrew faith. That faith had no priestesses at the time, so the fact that pagan religions did so was irrelevant. Why would Jews have cared about what pagans did? His limiting the gender of the apostles to men would have been a practical solution also so he could promote acceptance of his teachings by his followers since they were mostly Jewish. I think the real story lies with what happened after Jesus.

"Since all the apostles were Jewish males in a society where the status of a female was just above a slave, it's not surprising that none of the early Christian men felt compelled to ordain a woman. Women were inferior beings and therefore could not be in a leadership role. The same treatment of women by the Catholic Church has unfortunately continued beyond early Christian times. I remember when I was a boy; women had to have their heads covered before entering the church. They couldn't enter the sanctuary except for cleaning purposes. They couldn't read Scripture from the pulpit. They couldn't act as Mass servers, and they couldn't touch sacred items, such as the chalice. They couldn't sing in the church choir, and they couldn't distribute communion. Today they can do all those things, yet they still cannot be a priest.

"I was a boy no fewer than fifty years ago. So if the situation with regard to women was like that just *fifty* years ago, just think what it must have been like *two thousand* years ago!"

R.A. BROWN

Tommy took a sip of coffee and continued, "So the fact is simply this: Christ did not name a woman apostle. That's it! The Catholic Church's story is that the omission was on purpose, to exclude women forever from the priesthood. If the jury believes that, then the church has a good reason to do what they do. My story is that there were a number of other reasons why he did not name a woman as an apostle, any of which could explain his actions, and any of which could tilt the scales of justice in our favor. I like our odds. Their burden will be to prove their position in one way only, and we have the option to prove our position with one of many.

"There are a number of very sensible reasons why Jesus did what he did, and none of them meant to lead to the exclusion of women forever from the priesthood. I think the church is really stretching to come up with the 'he didn't do something on purpose' argument to justify two thousand years of sexual discrimination. Since they have no direct, divine revelation from the Scriptures, they're relying on divine revelation by omission. How silly is that?"

Tommy took a bite of a kolache and drank some more coffee and let everybody think about what he had said. Then he asked, "Are there any questions or comments?"

"I have a question," Rickie said. "Their story as you tell it seems to be somewhat circumspect. Is that all there is?"

"They have other arguments, but they're all used to support the basic premise that because Jesus didn't do something, he meant that it should last forever. Also, there's the fact that a pope, who is infallible when he speaks on Catholic Church doctrine, has said the same thing," Tommy answered.

"Do Catholics believe that, that a man is infallible?" Rickie asked.

"There are a billion Catholics in the world, and most of them believe that," Tommy replied.

"You're Catholic. Do you believe that?" Billie asked.

"It doesn't matter what I believe. The only thing that matters is what the jury believes," Tommy said.

Billie responded, "With all due respect, if the jury believes your story, then six or twelve people could make one billion Catholics hopping mad."

"Then one billion Catholics will just have to find a church that doesn't break the laws," Tommy said curtly. "Anybody else have a question?"

Rickie said, "I have one. Tommy, your story depends upon your interpretation of the religious explanation for an action of Jesus. To sell your story, you'll have to overturn two thousand years of Catholic teaching. You'll be fighting the Catholic Church on their own turf on issues that they know by heart. How are you going to do that?"

Tommy answered, "By showing their answers are illogical and simply don't make sense. It's like in any lawsuit: the story that makes the most sense based upon the facts will be the one the jury believes. A number of Christian faiths allow and even promote a female clergy. This is not something out of the realm of today's Christianity."

Tommy paused and asked, "Are there any other questions? Good, then let me summarize. Federal court has jurisdiction over the Catholic Church, and that is clear. What is not clear is whether we have the law on our side and so the odds are anywhere from fifty percent to one hundred percent our suit will be dismissed. However, and I will admit this is a big *however*, if we get the right judge and get it to the jury, we have an argument that could well succeed. Agreed?"

Everyone nodded their heads.

"Billie and Rickie, please draft the complaint on behalf of Aleksandra Kowalski alleging gender discrimination without just cause in refusing to allow her to attend the seminary. The defendants are the Archdiocese of Galveston-Houston and Cardinal Sierra. Silk, please review their draft and let me take a look at it this afternoon. I want to file it tomorrow morning if we can. Tim, in addition to the research on Alex, please get me a list of Catholic theologians and scholars, hopefully ordained, who have come out in opposition to the church's position on this issue. I suspect there may be a lot of them. Interview those that you can about why they disagree and their reasons for disagreement. Explain what the lawsuit is about and ask if they would be willing to testify on behalf of Alex.

"Also, I found out from my conversation with Father Damien there are psychologists and psychiatrists who do interviews with potential applicants to the seminary. Find out who they are in this archdiocese and ask them if they would be willing to interview Alex as if they were interviewing a male applicant and judge her accordingly. This is a hurdle all applicants to the seminary have to clear, and if we get by the gender disqualification, I don't want her being denied admittance on a technicality later."

Tim looked up from taking his notes and nodded.

"Any comments?" Tommy asked.

When nobody responded, Tommy said, "Good. Let's get going. I'll call Alex and tell her of our decision to proceed on her behalf."

Everyone pushed their chairs back, picked up their papers, and left the room to Tommy and his thoughts. The more he thought about it, the more he liked this lawsuit. He liked his story better than the church's story. But Billie's question kept bothering him. What did he believe? Did it matter? No, what mattered was the story, and his story made the most sense.

CHAPTER FOURTEEN

Tommy called Alex. "Hello, Alex, this is Tommy O'Reilly."

"Oh, hello, Mr. O'Reilly. I've been waiting for your call. What have you decided to do?"

"Alex, I have decided to take the case and represent you in your action against the Catholic Church. However, I feel it's my duty to warn you, if you have any reservations, speak up now. Otherwise, we intend to file the complaint as soon as we can, maybe even tomorrow morning."

"Mr. O'Reilly, I have absolutely no reservations! As I told you when we met, I have prayed about this decision for a very long time, and I believe God has chosen me to be one of his priests. Since we met, I have prayed continually that God would give you his direction on your choice. Whatever choice you made would be his decision, and I can accept that no matter what. Now that it's over with, I have no reservations about your decision to go ahead with the lawsuit. It's really God's will."

"Alex, alert your family and friends about the lawsuit before we file tomorrow. Tell them to be aware of anybody asking questions and not to answer any questions from anyone. And, Alex, prepare yourself for

R.A. BROWN

the most intense examination of your life. The church will certainly get into your background, but also the news media will be digging for every sordid detail of your life." He didn't mention that Prentice's people would also be asking questions, but if they reported back that the people they tried to talk to were not responsive, that would be a good thing.

"I've already talked to everyone I could think of," Alex answered. "They know what I'm doing, and they're supportive. I'm ready, and they're ready for whatever will come."

As he said his good-byes and promised to keep her posted every day on what he was doing, he hoped he was also ready for whatever was to come.

On Tuesday morning he read the complaint, and it was succinct and to the point. It alleged that the defendants were in violation of the Civil Rights Act of 1964 in denying Aleksandra Kowalski acceptance to St. John's seminary in Beaumont, Texas. The defendants were the Archdiocese of Galveston-Houston and the Archbishop of the Diocese, Cardinal Jorge Sierra. It was filed in the United States Federal Court, Southern District of Texas. It was filed electronically, and upon receipt by the District Court, the action was placed into the computer for a random draw of the judge to whom the case would be assigned. The name that came up was US Federal District Court Judge John Bateman. A summons was issued electronically back to the offices of the O'Reilly Law Group. Upon receipt, Betty Lincoln made a copy and gave it to the process server that the firm normally used. By two p.m. that afternoon, process was duly served upon His Eminence, Bishop Cardinal Jorge Sierra and the archdiocese. The wheels of justice were now in motion.

At four p.m. Eastern Standard Time in the city of Washington D.C., Monsignor Enrico Renzulli received a copy of the complaint from the office of the archdiocese. Monsignor Renzulli was the general counsel of the United States Conference of Catholic Bishops. The USCCB had jurisdiction over all lawsuits filed against the Catholic Church in any diocese in the United States, and Rick Renzulli was the man to defend and try any such cases.

Rick Renzulli read the complaint and called his adjunct into his office. "Father Murray, please start an immediate investigation on Aleksandra Kowalski, a resident of Houston, Texas, and Thomas Patrick O'Reilly, an attorney in the same town. I've sent you a copy of the complaint filed today in Houston federal court by e-mail. Read it, and it should give you all you need to know to form the basis of your investigation. If you have any questions, or if anything arises in your investigation that I should need to know about, please call me any time night or day on my cell phone. Also notify the Chairman of the Conference of Catholic Bishops and e-mail him a copy of the lawsuit with a copy to the Solicitor General at the Vatican."

"Yes, Monsignor, I'll get right to it, and I'll put a rush on it," Father Murray said and he left the office.

Monsignor Renzulli leaned back in his chair and stared out at the Capitol. He thought that this indeed was something new. Unlike the sex scandal cases that had taken most if not all of his time in the past several years, this had an element of interest; an action that, to his knowledge, had never been filed before. Something new was always interesting, but this probably would not last very long. After all, there was the First Amendment, which required the separation of church and state, and he could undoubtedly get this case dismissed on a motion for summary judgment. Nevertheless, he should be prepared to spend some time in the archbishop's residence in Houston. *That might not be all bad,* he thought. He would get a chance to get to know Archbishop Sierra better. He had only met him a few times, but for a bishop in the United States to be elevated to the rank of cardinal meant the archbishop was held in high regard in Rome, and church politics being what they were, it never hurt to have more friends in high places. Seeing it was late in the day, Monsignor Renzulli locked up his office and retired to his living quarters adjacent to the offices of the USCCB. While he ate he began developing a strategy for the new lawsuit. After all, this was a case the church could not afford to lose! This was not about money; it was about something much more important. It was about a fundamental way of life that had been in existence for *two thousand years*. He had better bring his A-game to this one, or he might be looking at being a pastor at a parish in the most godforsaken place in the world.

CHAPTER FIFTEEN

Enrico "Rick" Renzulli was a strikingly handsome man. He was tall, about six feet, and had a slim physique. His hair was coal black, and his complexion was dark, the result of his Italian heritage. He had a straight Roman nose, high cheekbones, and full, almost sensuous, lips. A bright smile with very white teeth was a startling contrast to his very dark eyes. He had worked in his parents' law office during the summer while in the high school seminary and had continued to work there during the summers while in collegiate seminary.

Although his desire to be a priest had only increased while at the seminary, Rick had also discovered something else while working the summers at the law firm. He also wanted to be a lawyer. After graduation and ordination, he requested the vocation office of the diocese to allow him to attend law school. Based upon his outstanding academic record and attitude, the diocese granted his request. He took the LSAT, and his score was high enough that he was accepted to Harvard. Again, due to his focus and mental ability, his academic excellence continued and he graduated in the top 10 percent of his law school class. After graduation he applied for and was accepted to study for a doctorate in canon law at the Holy See in Rome. After obtaining his PhD, he stayed in Rome and worked in the Vatican on legal affairs which affected the Catholic Church. In addition to English, he also became fluent in Italian and Latin.

Years later when the priest-related sex scandals broke in the United States, Rick was sent back to work with the USCCB in the defense of those cases. While initially he had directed local counsel in the church's defense, he soon began to participate in the trials themselves and became an adept litigator. Now in his mid-forties, he was recognized and highly regarded in both church canon law circles and civil law circles. Along with good genes, the years had been kind to him, and age seemed to enhance his physical appearance. In the few times he appeared in public without his Roman collar, people assumed he was in an exotic profession such as a Formula One racecar driver or even a professional polo player. In all respects, Enrico "Rick" Renzulli was a man who was on top of his game.

After thinking the matter over the previous night, Monsignor Renzulli walked into his office Wednesday morning with a decision. Again he called Father Murray into his office.

"Father, I want to file an answer in the Aleksandra Kowalski litigation Friday morning. I also want to file a motion for summary judgment and request an immediate hearing on the motion. I want to get this dismissed as soon as we can before it gains too much traction with the news media. It'll be bad enough as it is. The basis of the motion will be the church's rights under the First Amendment accompanied by a legal brief containing appropriate case and statutory law supporting the motion. We have argued First Amendment rights many times before, so all we should have to do is to tailor the brief to fit the specific facts of this case. I think it's important to strike quickly so that Mr. Thomas Patrick O'Reilly knows his opposition is well prepared for litigation. I think it'll also send the same message to the judge who'll be assigned the case. Let everybody involved know the Catholic Church is extremely serious about the defense of this lawsuit and we will not be a pushover, nor will we be railroaded into changing something that we have held sacred for our entire history. Can we get all the pleadings filed by Friday?"

"Yes, Monsignor, we can do it. We'll select local counsel today, send them our answer, motion, and brief by Thursday afternoon to be filed electronically Friday signed by you and local counsel. We will also have local counsel move to have you admitted to practice law in the Southern District of Texas for the purposes of this litigation. If I may say so, Monsignor, it'll be nice to have a case we can win after some of those we have been through lately."

"I hope that you're right, Father. I hope you're right," Monsignor Renzulli said quietly.

CHAPTER SIXTEEN

Betty greeted Tommy when he walked into the office Friday morning and said, "Good morning, boss. As we say in Navasota, you sure got a stick into a mess of rattlesnakes, but these rattlesnakes happen to be wearing crosses."

"After all these years, I think I'm beginning to understand 'Betty lingo,'" Tommy said with a smile. "I assume we have heard from the archdiocese?"

"Have we ever. They filed their answer this morning and e-mailed a copy to you. They also moved for summary judgment with an accompanying brief of thirty-five pages, which they also e-mailed to you. Their answer essentially said you are a liar, because they denied anything and everything that you said. Their motion and brief also said you don't know squat, because you have no business filing this lawsuit in federal court and the judge should throw it out right now!" Betty exclaimed.

"How do you know this, Betty?"

"'cause Willis told me so."

"And perhaps you're paraphrasing just a little?" Tommy teased.

"No, boss, I'm telling you like it is," Betty said firmly.

Tommy went into his office, went to his e-mails, and read the pleadings submitted by the defendants. He was impressed by the brief and the underlying arguments and law that supported it. He also read the motion to admit Monsignor Enrico Renzulli to the bar for the specific purpose of this litigation and the résumé of the monsignor that had been attached to the motion, and he had to admit that he was impressed. He picked up the phone and called Gerald Grant and asked him to step into his office.

Gerald was a brilliant lawyer, one of the top graduates of his law school class. However, Gerald had a problem that prevented major law firms from offering him a position after an interview; he stuttered badly. Whenever Gerald talked in front of a group or was under pressure, he stuttered to a point that his listener or listeners wanted to finish his sentences for him. It would not be possible to put Gerald in front of a judge, jury, or even a client. This affliction did not prevent Gerald from writing, however. Tommy had offered Gerald a job to do one thing, and that was to research and write legal briefs. What Gerald couldn't say well, he could write. And at that he was exceptional.

"Wha-wha-what's up, Tommy?" Gerald asked as he walked into his office.

"You may have heard we have filed a lawsuit against the Catholic Church," Tommy replied.

"Ye-ye-yes, I know about that. Be-Be-Betty says she is go-go-going to install a lightning rod on the office," Gerald said, smiling.

Tommy smiled back. "Gerald, I'm going to e-mail you our complaint, their answer, and motion for summary judgment, along with their brief supporting the motion. Please get with Rickie and Billie on their research on our legal standing to bring suit in federal court. Please prepare a brief in response to their motion."

How soo-soo-soo … quick do you want this?" Gerald asked.

"As soon as you can deliver it. I want them to know we're as prepared as they are. If they want to fast-track this, we're ready to go. Oh, Gerald, their brief is thirty-five pages. Try to make our brief thirty-six. Also, on your way out, ask Betty to notify Judge Bateman's office that we have no objection to the motion to admit Monsignor Renzulli. I know the motion is perfunctory and will be granted anyway, but it's always helpful to appear agreeable to the judge."

Every Friday afternoon, Rebecca Gomez, a court clerk in the US district federal court, would take an hour after work and review the cases that had been filed during the week. She had an agreement with Bruce Wilkes, a reporter for the *Houston Chronicle,* to send him, in return for fifty dollars, any noteworthy cases filed during the week that he could use for the "City and State" section of the *Chronicle.* After she had read the complaint and answer in the Kowalski litigation, she picked up the phone and called Bruce and was put through immediately.

"This may be worth a hundred dollars," she said.

"Oh, really? Let's hear what you've got."

After she had summarized the complaint and answer, Bruce said, "E-mail me what you've got. If it is what you say it is, you've got a hundred dollars plus a dozen roses."

Once Bruce Wilkes had received Rebecca's e-mail, he thought he might earn a headline for the "City and State" section of the Saturday *Chronicle.* After he had written his story, he sent it to his editor, who had sent it to the editor-in-chief of the *Chronicle,* Mike Alford. Alford was an old newspaper man who knew a good story when he saw it. Once he read it, he decided to reference it on the front page of the *Chronicle* itself as "Local woman sues Catholic Church to become a priest, see section B for the story" where it was then featured in a headline. The paper went to press that night, and it was delivered to the newsstands and the distributors for home deliveries the next morning. On Saturday morning, there it was; the lead story in an otherwise dull weekend edition.

CHAPTER SEVENTEEN

At the same time Friday afternoon that Rebecca reviewed cases filed during the week for newsworthy articles, Judge John Bateman met with his staff attorneys to go over cases filed during the week and to which he had been assigned. First up were the criminal cases that invariably clogged his docket because of the immediate attention the law required him to give them. Last up was the civil docket.

After they had gone through the civil cases to which he had been assigned during the week, Dick Cole, his lead staff attorney, said, "Your Honor, I have saved the best for last. Alexandra Kowalski has sued the Catholic Church under the Civil Rights Act of 1964, requesting a mandatory injunction to allow her into the seminary, so that she might study to become ordained as a Catholic priest. She has also requested a jury trial for determination of the facts reserving the question of equitable relief for your determination.

"The defendants are the Archdiocese of Galveston-Houston and Bishop Cardinal Jorge Sierra. This case was filed on Tuesday, and today we received an answer stating a general denial to all claims. The defendants also filed a motion for summary judgment to dismiss the

R.A. BROWN

action accompanied by a legal brief of the law. I will also point out that neither party has requested any discovery."

"No discovery requests? That's unusual," Judge Bateman said. John Bateman had a reputation for being decisive and moving his docket along as fast as he could. His pet peeve was the plaintiff's attorney who filed a lawsuit and then spent the next two years issuing legal interrogatories and taking depositions in an attempt to prove his case. Woe be to the attorney who, after filing a lawsuit, went on a fishing expedition to try to prove the case he had filed.

"Who is the plaintiff's attorney?" Judge Bateman asked.

"Tommy O'Reilly," Cole responded.

"Oh, boy," Judge Bateman said. "Tommy O'Reilly doesn't like to waste time, and this sounds like a case he would file. Who's the attorney for the defendants?"

Dick Cole responded reading from his notes. "A local firm of Colby and Colby is acting as local counsel for Monsignor Enrico Renzulli. The monsignor is the general counsel for the United States Conference of Catholic Bishops and has assumed defense of the archdiocese and the archbishop. Colby and Colby have moved to have the monsignor admitted to the Southern District of Texas for the purposes of this litigation.

"To support their motion, they attached Monsignor Renzulli's curriculum vitae. He has a Harvard law degree and also a Ph.D. in Canon law from the Vatican. Mr. O'Reilly's firm called earlier and said they had no objection to the motion to admit Monsignor Renzulli. The defendants have also requested an expedited hearing on their motion for summary judgment."

"Please prepare an order with my signature granting the motion to admit, and e-mail a copy to all counsel. In the meantime, we will await Mr. O'Reilly's response to the motion for summary judgment, but knowing O'Reilly, he also will want to move this along. I suspect this is a case that will be attracting the news media. We'll have to remind everyone that there will be no cameras allowed in the courtroom.

If that's it, then, I'll see you boys Monday morning. Have a good weekend," Judge Bateman said cordially.

"You too, Your Honor," they replied.

Judge Bateman took off his judicial robes, hung them in his closet, and left his office to go to the parking lot. John Bateman had been appointed to the federal bench by President Clinton after a distinguished career as a litigator for a major Houston law firm. He had been active in the Democratic Party since college, and despite some minor opposition from a handful of Republican senators, he had been readily approved by the senate since both Republican senators from Texas had supported his appointment. During his years on the bench, he had developed a reputation as a progressive judge.

On his drive home from downtown Houston to the Woodlands, an affluent residential community north of Houston, he thought about the Kowalski case. If he had been a Catholic, he might have had an issue as to whether to recuse himself and have another judge appointed. But he wasn't a Catholic, and in fact he had no religious preference at all since he was not religious in any way. While his gut told him that something had to start the universe and all that was in it, he did not or could not believe in the God of the Scriptures.

If there really was a God who was all powerful and all loving, he would not allow the terrible suffering of humans that existed in the world today. How could someone who loved people so much hurt people the way he did? If he was all powerful, he obviously could stop the pain and suffering immediately. It did not make sense to worship a God who would allow all of the terrible things that he allowed. He did not often think about what, if anything, happened after death because he didn't have any answers. And for someone who was used to having answers that made him uncomfortable. He was looking forward to this case because he would have a chance to assess some people who, at least in their own minds, were sure about those answers. *This promises to be an interesting case,* he thought.

CHAPTER EIGHTEEN

Saturday morning Michael once again read the article in the Houston Chronicle. This made him angrier, more so than when he had first read the article. In fact, he was incensed! He knew as well as anybody, maybe more so, what it took to be a priest. How could a woman presume to be qualified and acceptable to be ordained a priest? This was heresy, a crime against the church, which in the old days would have been dealt with summarily by first torture, and then death. *Even though those were appropriate actions in the eyes of God,* he thought. *The church would not undertake those measures today.*

Holy Mother Church had gotten soft with her political correctness, and he longed for the old days when the church was feared and all were respectful. He took a deep breath and tried to calm himself. He knew Monsignor Renzulli's reputation was that of an excellent priest and an excellent lawyer. Surely he, with God's help, would be able to prevent such a travesty. Michael also knew that in his own position, he would have a front row seat to the proceedings. He would watch carefully as the lawsuit proceeded, and if it started going badly against the church, he would be prepared to do whatever God told him had to be done. With that, he felt better, stood up, smoothed down any wrinkles in his cassock with both hands, and went to Mass.

CHAPTER NINETEEN

By Monday morning the news of the lawsuit had gone national, both in print and on television. All news organizations reported that the Archdiocese of Galveston-Houston had refused to comment on existing litigation. Calls to the O'Reilly Law Group had not been returned. A few noted this was unusual for a plaintiff's attorney not to seek publicity for himself, his client, and his case.

The Wall Street Journal had a front-page lead article headlined "God's Law versus Federal Law." The reporter, Carolyn Rhymes, had interviewed theologians and Catholic scholars about the basis of the church's view of the matter. She had interviewed practicing attorneys and constitutional law professors concerning the legal positions, both of the plaintiff and the defendants. The article concluded that it was groundbreaking litigation and however the case turned out in trial court, it would probably have to be resolved at the appellate level.

The New York Times also had a front page article, and its reporter had also interviewed legal and church scholars. After dutifully reporting the opinions of those interviewed and in keeping with its progressive style, the reporter suggested that the Catholic Church was a sexist organization run by stubborn old men and that the right of the individual, in this case a woman, outweighed the Neanderthal attitude of the church.

Fox News had devoted fifteen minutes in its morning segment on the litigation. At midday, they had two different practicing attorneys with opposing view points involved in a debate with one another as to the merits of each position. Monday evening, a commentator who had an hour show every night during the week concluded his program with a discussion of the case. After stating he had been educated in the parochial school system and was a practicing Catholic, he concluded with his opinion that the constitutional guarantee of the freedom of religion prevented the Catholic Church from any interference by the state in the church's ecclesiastical rules.

MSNBC not surprisingly took a view opposite that of Fox News. One of their commentators, who also had an hourly show every week night, also discussed the issues raised in Kowalski versus the Archdiocese of Galveston-Houston. That reporter opined that no one or nothing was above the law, and as such the Catholic Church could not operate outside the law. The law was clear that the discrimination of women was illegal in the United States, and the church could either abide by the law or get out.

When Tommy reached his office that morning and pulled into the parking lot, there to greet him were six news trucks with the requisite satellite dishes on the roofs. Reporters with microphones accompanied by film crews rushed up to him as he exited his truck. They were yelling questions at him, sticking microphones in his face, but he was able to brush past them into his office.

Betty met him with, "Good morning, boss. Larry King's representative called. You know the guy with the suspenders as wide as my hand and colored like a brocaded quilt? They want to know if you will appear on his show."

"Betty, you know my rules on the media," Tommy answered. "No interviews whatsoever and no discussion about pending litigation.

I might, and I repeat, *might*, meet with the press after the jury has reached a decision and has been dismissed."

"Yeah I know, boss, but I was hoping you might make an exception in this case. It would get Leroy and Benjamin to watch something besides *Dancing with the Stars*."

"Sorry, Betty, no can do. Go get Leroy and Benjamin some more Astros tickets." Tommy chuckled and started toward his office.

Before he reached it, Betty said, "There was a call that was perhaps more serious boss." He turned around and saw Betty wasn't smiling. "What was the call about Betty?"

She said, "Maybe it was nothing but the caller said 'God promises immediate death to all heretics and those who support their heresy!'"

"Who was it, Betty?"

"I don't know, it was a male with a low voice, and the caller ID was blocked," she replied calmly.

After a moment Tommy said, "Betty, it was probably some crank, but I want those news folks off our property any way. Please call Sergeant Roy Yardley of the Houston Police Department. Ask him if he can assign off-duty police officers to be here twenty-four-seven. He can arrange the shifts however he wishes, but I would like to have two officers here at all times. My first request is to have the officers remind the news media that this is private property and they are not allowed on the premises.

"For the night shifts I want them to be on the lookout for any crazies who might have vindictive or destructive intentions toward our property. Also, tell Roy that whatever the going rate is, I'll double it. Also, call Alex and see if the news media has uncovered the nunnery where she lives. If they haven't found her, tell her to stay inside and lie low."

He grabbed a cup of Camp 4 coffee and went into his office. He checked his computer and saw he had an e-mail from Gerald Grant that had attached a rough draft of the response brief to the motion for summary judgment filed by the Catholic Church. Gerald had obviously worked over the weekend, and Tommy began to review the draft.

He noticed that Gerald had copied Silk as well, and he assumed Silk was reviewing it as he was. That afternoon, Tommy, Silk, and Gerald got together and went over Tommy's and Silk's comments. By the end of the afternoon, they were comfortable with their response and its supporting law. It was also one-half page longer than the defendants' brief, and they decided to file their response the next morning with a request for an expedited hearing on the defendants' motion. They were as anxious to get it heard as Renzulli was.

When Tommy left that evening, he noticed that the HPD officers were in place and had moved the news media from the property. As Tommy drove off, three news trucks followed him to the Towers of Houston, where the security there prevented the trucks from going onto the property. *The right of privacy is special,* Tommy thought, but it sure did cost him a lot of money and effort to maintain his.

CHAPTER TWENTY

Monday night, Michael watched the cable news channels, and he was infuriated by the commentary. *How dare these idiots challenge my church on one of its fundamental principles? The Catholic Church was God's representative on earth, and what the church said has been divinely revealed by God. If the Catholic Church says that the priesthood is reserved for males only, then that has to be God's will. How ridiculous to even consider that a man-made law of the government, any government, could overrule the will of God.*

What was worse, it appeared a large number of intelligent people were strongly against the church on this issue. He felt this was starting to get out of hand, and once again he took a deep breath and tried to calm himself. Nothing had happened so far, just a lot of noise about the lawsuit. The archdiocese had filed a motion for summary judgment, which he knew to be similar to a motion to dismiss. He would be there to watch the proceedings, and certainly that motion would be granted and all of this would be over and soon forgotten. But what if it didn't get dismissed? He needed to be prepared in case

God directed him to stop this heretic and her heretic lawyer. After all, he *had* warned the lawyer. He began to develop a plan in his mind, and the more he thought about it, the more he liked it.

CHAPTER TWENTY-ONE

Tuesday morning, Monsignor Renzulli was enjoying a cup of cappuccino while reading his e-mail. He had moved into the guest quarters of Archbishop Sierra's residence. The residence was attached to the offices of the archbishop, and Monsignor Renzulli occupied an office set aside for traveling dignitaries. That morning a response to his motion for summary judgment had been filed with the court and a copy was e-mailed to him from the O'Reilly Law Group. He had just finished reading it. He was impressed by the legal argument, but not surprised. He had expected O'Reilly to argue that the right to practice one's religion was not guaranteed if the practice of that religion otherwise violated US law. Whoever had written the brief had done an excellent job of presenting the plaintiff's position, and he was sure O'Reilly didn't have the legal acumen to do so.

He read in great detail the investigation reports on O'Reilly and Aleksandra Kowalski. Kowalski, he had to grudgingly admit to himself, would be an excellent candidate for the priesthood if her name had been Alexander and not Aleksandra. Nothing was there that would be helpful. But O'Reilly was a different matter.

It appeared to Monsignor Renzulli that O'Reilly had never really earned anything; it just seemed he was always in the right spot at the right time. Enrico Renzulli believed that those who relied on luck for their achievements would inevitably run out of luck at some point. Although O'Reilly had a high success rate in the cases he tried, it did not match with his mediocre academic record. He obviously wasn't dazzling juries and judges with his brilliance, so it had to be something else. He needed to meet O'Reilly and take a measure of the man.

Then he got an idea, the type of idea that he prided himself on. While Monsignor Renzulli was confident in his motion for summary judgment and the law that backed it up, the response by The O'Reilly Law Group was very well written, and the judge might go either way. Since he always tried to be prepared for any contingency, if the judge ruled in favor of the plaintiff, then he had to be prepared to try the case. He knew by experience that a critical part of his trial strategy would be to understand and anticipate what the opposing attorney might do. The local rules of the Southern District required counsel for both parties to have a meeting prior to trial to discuss any potential settlement. Although it was required, the rules did not specify a time frame in which the meeting should occur. Monsignor Renzulli thought that the time to do that was now.

CHAPTER TWENTY-TWO

"My, my, my, said the spider to the fly, come see what I have for you," Betty chimed to Tommy on Wednesday morning. "The monsignor has requested a meeting with you at the offices of the archbishop, or if you are not comfortable with that, then any other place of your choosing."

"Has he suggested a time for the meeting, Betty?" Tommy asked.

"He said to leave that up to you, but anytime Friday would be convenient for him," Betty replied.

"Friday morning at ten a.m. will be convenient for me," Tommy said. "I wonder what he wants."

"I don't know. I talked to his assistant, Father Michael Murray. He said it was in conformance with the court rules requiring settlement discussions. He said Monsignor Renzulli thought this would be a good time to do so since there was a 'lull in the action.' His words, not mine."

Tommy thought a moment and mused, "I still wonder what he wants. This meeting cannot possibly be about a settlement when there cannot be a basis for a settlement. Alex is either admitted to the seminary or she isn't. There is no possible middle ground for a settlement. There must be a hidden agenda of some kind. Oh, well, I'll just have to see what the good monsignor has on his mind. Please set it up for Friday, Betty."

Tommy then went into his office and began to review the written transcripts of interviews of certain individuals by an associate of Tim Prentice, Tom Johnson. The interviews were with Catholic Church scholars and theologians who did not support the church's position for a male-only priesthood. There were a number of them, and Johnson had indicated he could interview more, but he had limited the initial group in geography first to Texas, and then the Southwest. All of the priests who had been interviewed had been defrocked because of their position on this issue. Tommy had to think about whether a defrocked priest would be a good witness in the eyes of the jury or not.

On the one hand, they had made a tremendous sacrifice to speak what they believed to be true, the sacrifice being their vocation. On the other hand, Monsignor Renzulli would be able to impeach their testimony as the ranting of a rogue group. He undoubtedly would point out that, of the many thousands of priests in the United States, only a few have adopted a position contrary to the Vatican. Two priests that Prentice's associate had uncovered who had been covertly championing a change in the gender issue would not testify. They were also out of the jurisdiction of the Southern District's subpoena power, so Tommy could not force them to do so. But he would not do that in any event, since he was reluctant to put on hostile witnesses to support his case in chief.

The scholars and theologians who weren't priests were another matter. They were very vocal about the lack of divine revelation to support the church's stand. They were willing to testify because they had written articles and even books on the issue. Tommy knew, however, that for each witness Tommy put on, Renzulli would be able to put on two or more to counter his witnesses. This would result in a trial of competing experts put on by both sides, which could take weeks or even months to finish depending on how many witnesses each side would wish to call.

Tommy knew also that Judge Bateman would not be happy about or even agree to a trial that long. Then he began to get an idea. It would be brazen, but it could work. It would certainly shorten the trial to a day or two and might accelerate a trial setting. It was a lot easier to get a two-day trial on the docket then a two-week trial. He decided to talk to Silk about it and see what he thought. But the more he thought about it, the more he liked it.

CHAPTER TWENTY-THREE

The black Lincoln town car pulled up to the offices of the archdiocese at five minutes until ten Friday morning. Manuel was driving as he did for Tommy and the other attorneys to take them to the courthouses and other meetings around town. Tommy had remembered Joe Bob telling him, "Manny is blank as a check, but he can drive like a pro. Dumb as he is, he's smart enough not to talk about what he hears." He wasn't any smarter than when he had driven for Joe Bob, but he was still an excellent driver and very dependable.

"Manny, find a coffee shop nearby, and I'll call you on your cell phone when I'm ready to leave," Tommy said.

"Yes, sir, Mr. O'Reilly," Manuel said as he pulled away from the curb.

The archdiocese was headquartered in a three-story white building and, with the adjacent cathedral, took up a whole city block near downtown Houston.

He walked into a prestigious and professionally appointed lobby and up to a young priest seated at a large dark wooden desk.

"What may I do for you sir?" the priest asked affably.

Tommy said, "My name is Thomas Patrick O'Reilly," and handed the man his card. "I have an appointment with Monsignor Renzulli, who is a visiting prelate from Chicago."

The priest looked down at his card and then up at Tommy, and his expression turned visibly colder. "Have a seat over there, and I will tell the monsignor you are here."

Apparently this priest reads newspapers, Tommy thought.

He walked over to where the priest had pointed and heard the priest say into a phone, "Please tell Monsignor Renzulli that *he's* here."

Tommy chuckled to himself and sat in a plush, soft leather chair and took note of the surroundings. On one wall was the most magnificent crucifix he thought he had ever seen. Another wall had a picture of Pope Benedict XVI and on another a picture of Bishop Cardinal Sierra.

The coffee table in front of him had numerous Catholic publications and news periodicals. The current issue of *Time Magazine* caught his attention. The cover had a cross that was burning with the caption, "Is the Catholic Church being forced into the new age?" As Tommy reached for the magazine to thumb through the article, a priest different from the one at the reception walked up to him and curtly said, "Follow me." It occurred to Tommy that no one so far had offered to shake his hand.

He was ushered into an office that contained four low, plush leather chairs that looked like little brothers to the couch he had sat on in the lobby. They framed a low, bare coffee table.

The priest pointed to the chairs and said, "Monsignor Renzulli will be with you as soon as he is able," and rudely turned and left the room without another word.

The archdiocese must have a shortage of water, coffee, or soft drinks, Tommy thought with a smile.

A few minutes later a slim man in his forties walked in. He wore a priest's cassock, but instead of the white Roman collar, he wore purple, which signified the rank of a monsignor. He had dark hair, a dark complexion, and brown eyes. Tommy was not one to dwell on the looks of other men, but it did occur to him that this monsignor would have no issues if he ever decided to break his vow of celibacy.

As far as Monsignor Renzulli's initial impression of Tommy, the first thing he noticed were the pale blue eyes framed by a dark complexion. *He must have a lot of time in the sun or tanning booths,* he thought, but the lack of any wrinkles told him his coloring was probably natural. His hair was thick and white and complimented the white smile Tommy gave him as he said hello. He had a tall, broad-shouldered, and narrow-waisted athletic build handsomely set off by a dark-gray handmade suit.

After they had shaken hands and made introductions, the monsignor offered Tommy a chair, which Tommy took, and the monsignor sat down in another one across from Tommy with the low coffee table in between.

Tommy decided to get right to the point. "What did you have in mind to discuss, Monsignor?"

Monsignor Renzulli replied, "A meeting to discuss possible settlement is required by the local rules. I thought this would be a good time to get together."

"We both know that won't be possible, unless you can agree that my client is eligible to attend the seminary," Tommy responded. "There can be no other resolution."

Monsignor Renzulli put his hands flat down on the table and leaned forward. "Not possible," he said firmly. "Not now, not ever."

Tommy shrugged his shoulders and said, "Fortunately, that decision will not be made by you or the church you represent. That will be entrusted to an unbiased jury of Aleksandra's peers."

"Are you not getting ahead of yourself, Tommy?" Monsignor Renzulli said smugly. "If the judge rules in my favor on my motion for summary judgment, and I believe he will, then there will be no facts to determine, and therefore no trial. So the decision of the church will remain as it is now, no women priests, not now, not ever!"

Tommy did not like Renzulli. He thought he was condescending and arrogant and any further discussion about a settlement was a waste of time. "First of all, Judge Bateman still has to rule, and I like our odds," Tommy replied firmly. "Second, only my friends can call me Tommy," he said as he started to stand up from his chair.

Rick Renzulli realized that he was making O'Reilly angry, and he didn't want him to get up and leave. He needed to talk to O'Reilly more to acquire an understanding of the man, which is really why he had called him here.

"Okay, Mr. O'Reilly, please calm down. I did not mean to offend you, and you are right. We may or may not have a trial. And that, as you have said, is out of our hands," Monsignor Renzulli said pleasingly. "Please, Mr. O'Reilly, may I offer you a cappuccino?"

Tommy took a deep breath and said, "Yes, a cappuccino would be nice. Thank you."

After the coffee had been served, Monsignor Renzulli asked, "How is your cappuccino?"

"I like cappuccino, and this is very good. Is this part of your influence in the headquarters here? You have an Italian name, and I thought maybe you brought a special recipe," Tommy replied conversationally.

"No, no nothing like that, I'm afraid. This is the standard fare in the archdiocese headquarters. But I offered you a cappuccino because I assumed you would have appreciation for all things Italian with an Italian mother," Renzulli stated.

"How did you know I had an Italian mother?" Tommy said somewhat guardedly.

Renzulli knew he had made a slip and had said something he didn't mean to say. "I know a few things about you. Not much, but a few things. For instance, I know you're Catholic. Your father was Irish and has passed away, and your mother is of Italian heritage and still with us. That's all," Renzulli lied.

Tommy had a feeling Renzulli knew a lot more about him than he was admitting, since any investigation the church had run would not stop just with his parents.

"I don't think you're being completely forthright Monsignor," Tommy said smiling. "I believe your investigators would have uncovered a lot more about me than just that."

"Well, yes, I must admit that I do know a bit more. I find it useful to know all that I can about opposing counsel. I like to know whom I'm up against. Don't you?" asked Monsignor Renzulli.

Tommy wanted to say he couldn't care less about focusing on opposing counsel because nobody would tell the story better than he could, but instead said, "Oh, I don't know. I suppose I'm more interested in the jury and the witnesses."

Monsignor Renzulli took a sip of his cappuccino, set the cup down, and said, "I notice you did not disagree when I said you are Catholic. As a Catholic, don't you feel a conflict of interest in representing the plaintiff in this lawsuit?"

"Not really," Tommy said. "I believe in the core doctrine of the Catholic Church, which is the teaching of Jesus as revealed by the Scriptures. That does not include the man-made rules of the cardinals and popes, which go beyond what can be considered the word of God."

Renzulli stiffened and said, "I assume you can give me an example."

"There are many examples, but let me give you one near and dear to my heart," Tommy answered.

"Please do so," Monsignor Renzulli replied, frowning.

"God gave Moses and the Hebrews the Ten Commandments, and the seventh one said, 'Thou shall not commit adultery.' God being God, he could've said anything he wanted to say. He could have easily said, 'thou shalt not commit premarital sex' or 'sex outside of marriage.' But he didn't. He said not to commit adultery, which is defined as sex between two married people not married to each other. If God had said 'Thou shalt not have sex outside of marriage,' then he would have covered premarital sex, extramarital sex, and adultery. But he didn't.

He limited the ban just to adultery. The church has expanded the seventh commandment to prohibit any sex outside of marriage."

"You have an interesting interpretation of the Bible, Mr. O'Reilly," Monsignor Renzulli said. "The church believes it has been divinely revealed that the purpose of sex is for procreation, and that would limit sex to two people who are married to one another. Since recreational sex is not for the purpose of procreation, any practice of that would be outside the will of God."

"Once again, God did not say that," Tommy said, smiling, "you and other men in the church did."

Renzulli thought, *How could anyone have such an absurd interpretation of the seventh commandment? No wonder he thinks women can and should be priests.*

"Are you familiar with the term 'cafeteria Catholic'?" Monsignor Renzulli asked.

Tommy shook his head, and the monsignor continued.

"A cafeteria Catholic is one who professes to be a Catholic but picks and chooses what teachings of the church he wishes to accept, much as one picks and chooses what he wishes to eat in a cafeteria. To be a Catholic, one must accept all teachings of the church. If he cannot accept even one church teaching, then he cannot call himself Catholic. This is particularly true with respect to dogma concerning faith and morals about which the pope has spoken and is in such matters infallible, such as the dogma concerning priests."

Aha, Tommy thought, *now we're getting to the heart of the matter.* "Let's talk about papal infallibility, Monsignor Renzulli. A number of the Catholic theologians and scholars, who we have interviewed for our case, tell me that the doctrine was not taught until 1870. If indeed the pope is infallible when he speaks on faith and morals, his infallibility didn't just start in 1870. It, by definition, had to have been there always. Why did it take so long to recognize papal infallibility if it was so obvious?"

Monsignor Renzulli just looked at him, so Tommy continued, "Those same theologians and scholars tell me that the First Vatican Council, which initiated the doctrine of papal infallibility in 1870, was convened by Pope Pius IX, who, by most accounts I am told, was mentally unstable. On the first ballot, 20 percent of the bishops were against instituting the doctrine of infallibility of the pope. In order to be valid dogma, my experts tell me, the doctrine, whatever it is, has to be divinely revealed and to have been taught by the church since the time of Christ.

"The fact that 20 percent of the bishops did not agree with it initially would say that papal infallibility had not been universally taught or universally believed since the time of Christ. It took eighty-three sessions to finally obtain concurrence, which says there were a lot of issues among the bishops with the mandate."

Monsignor Renzulli took a sip of cappuccino and put his cup down. "Almost 100 years later," he said, "The Second Vatican Council took the issue up and concurred unanimously with the mandate," he said.

Tommy replied, "I'm told that the same Second Vatican Council also repealed what had been taught by the same Pope Pius IX, who initiated the mandate of papal infallibility in the first place. His teachings that were repealed included slavery not being at odds with the teaching of the Catholic Church and that capitalism was a sin."

"When the Pius IX said those things, he was not speaking on faith and morals," Monsignor Renzulli replied firmly. "To be infallible, the pope has to speak 'ex-cathedra' or 'from the chair on faith and morals.' The church disagreed with what Pius IX said because he had not spoken ex-cathedra on faith and morals. They were merely opinions that he held."

Tommy looked at Monsignor Renzulli in amazement. "Slavery is not a moral issue?"

When Renzulli chose not to answer, Tommy continued, "If I understand you correctly, Monsignor, you look at what a pope says on faith and morals and choose either to believe it or not depending upon your rationalization of how he thought about it before he said it? If a pope says something you agree with, then it is must be from *the chair*. If you don't agree with it, then it must be an *opinion?*"

Tommy shook his head from side to side and said "So who's the cafeteria Catholic now, Monsignor Renzulli?" in a lilting tone he normally saved for cross-examination.

After a long silence with each staring into the other's eyes, Tommy said, "Look Monsignor Renzulli, we're getting into the very issues we'll get into at trial to determine whether or not the church has a reasonable basis for not allowing women to be priests. There is no sense in further debating anything here. I'm not going to convince you, and you're not going to convince me of anything. If Judge Bateman sustains your motion and throws us out, that's it. If not, we have a trial. We can each put on ten experts who will offer opposing opinions about the validity of the church's position on male-only priests. A trial like that could take weeks. I notice you did not ask for any discovery, and I haven't either. We both know what the other's position will be at trial so I assume you believe as I do there is no need for discovery. Correct?"

Renzulli nodded his head in the affirmative.

"I also believe that you wish a quick trial setting if it comes to that. Is that correct?"

"Yes, that's correct," Monsignor Renzulli said.

"You're new to this jurisdiction, but I can tell you that getting on Judge Bateman's docket quickly will be problematic if we have to schedule a trial for as long as I described. But I have a proposition that could and should get us on an accelerated docket if you would like to hear it," Tommy said.

"What's your proposal?" Monsignor Renzulli asked guardedly.

"I'll put on two witnesses only, Ms. Kowalski, plus a psychiatrist or psychologist whom the archdiocese uses to screen potential seminarians. The second witness is important because I wouldn't wish to succeed in court and have the archdiocese disqualify Ms. Kowalski on a technicality. She has not taken the interview yet, but I also agree to put the examiner on, whatever the opinion. That's how confident I am that Ms. Kowalski is as qualified as any candidate the examiner will have interviewed except for her gender. In return, you put on Bishop Cardinal Sierra, and that's it."

"If I understand you correctly, you will be relying solely upon your cross-examination of Archbishop Sierra to prove the church's position is unreasonable. You'll have no direct testimony from expert witnesses on this issue, correct?" Monsignor Renzulli said.

"That's correct. And you will put on no expert witnesses to support his opinion. We will both tell Judge Bateman that there will only be three witnesses in total. That's my proposal. That should allow for a trial, including jury selection, of two, maybe three, days. With all the publicity surrounding this lawsuit, Judge Bateman may have an incentive to find those two or three days on his docket as soon as can," Tommy said.

What an idiot, Monsignor Renzulli thought. He thinks he's smart enough to cross-examine Sierra and make his case against the church. Renzulli had spent several nights with Jorge Sierra and had found him to be extremely intelligent and knowledgeable about the church's position on this issue and all Scriptures in general. Jorge *Sierra will eat this guy up. This is too easy,* he thought. He had Tommy O'Reilly just where he wanted him.

"I agree," Monsignor Renzulli said.

Tommy said, "Okay, we're agreed. I will see you when your motion is set on the docket. If you win your motion, that will be it. If I win, we will tell the judge about our agreement. Do I need to confirm this in an e-mail, or can I count your word as a monsignor?"

Monsignor Renzulli looked at him and said dryly, "You can count on the word of a monsignor, but I will confirm it in an e-mail. I only have your word as a lawyer."

They said their good-byes with only the briefest of civility. Tommy exited the headquarters of the archdiocese and called Manny to pick him up. While waiting on the sidewalk he thought, *That was too easy.* He had Monsignor Renzulli just where he wanted him.

CHAPTER TWENTY-FOUR

When Manuel dropped Tommy at the office, Tommy noticed that the off-duty police officers were still there, but there was only one satellite news truck parked in the street. He thought the major networks had decided to pool resources and had picked one to remain on site in case Tommy agreed to an interview. *They'll have a long wait,* Tommy thought. Tommy walked into the reception area, and despite being the lunch hour, Betty was still at her desk. He wondered whether she ever ate or slept, because it seemed that she was always here, no matter the time.

"Hello boss. You look dry."

"Yes. So what?"

"So you must have held your own in the pissing contest."

"I wore a raincoat. Is Silk in, or is he at lunch?" Tommy asked.

"Willis is in. He wanted to hear how your meeting went. Do you want me to send him in?"

"Yes, milady," Tommy said with a slight bow before walking to his office. Before he entered his office, he turned to Betty and said, "Oh, and see what the officers out front want to eat and please have it delivered."

When Willis walked into Tommy's office, Tommy said simply, "He took the deal."

"No way! He didn't even want to think about it?" Willis asked.

"No, he probably thinks Sierra will carve me into little pieces. He probably thinks I'm an idiot for even suggesting the deal," Tommy said.

"He just might be right. Sierra has probably forgotten more about Catholic teaching than you will ever know," Willis replied.

"Yes, he has, but I don't think he'll eat me up," Tommy responded. "The jurors won't be theologians or scholars, just folks like me. I'll be asking questions in their terms, and he'll be responding as a theologian. Remember, it comes down to whether it makes sense or not, and if I don't think it makes sense, I think I can convince the jury that it doesn't make sense. By the way, have you talked to Dr. Turner yet?"

Prentice's group had contacted and interviewed one psychiatrist and two psychologists that the archdiocese used to screen applicants to the seminary. Two had declined to interview Alex and testify at trial because they did not want to get crosswise with the archdiocese. The third, Dr. Sylvia Turner, had readily agreed to do so, and Tommy had asked Silk to meet with her and talk to her.

"Yes, Tommy, I met with Dr. Turner while you were at the archdiocese. She is head of the Department of Psychology at St. Thomas College. She had been selected to interview applicants to the seminary because Archbishop Sierra thought it important to have a woman's viewpoint, which might lead to a different impression of the applicants.

"She told me that her income or position is not dependent on doing work for the archdiocese. Everyone she has deemed appropriate to enter the seminary has been admitted. Twice, applicants whom Dr. Turner felt had issues that would be detrimental to the applicant being an effective priest but had been approved by another interviewer, were ultimately turned down.

"She also said that she has the highest regard for Archbishop Sierra. He is a man with the highest integrity and morals and a man she feels is not bound to some of the conventions of the church, as her selection and appointment to interview the seminarian applicants suggests. Once Sierra accepted a married Episcopal priest and ordained him into the Catholic Church. Episcopalians also have women priests, but she is sure that he would not do the same for a female."

Interesting piece of information, Tommy thought, and made a mental note. "Can we trust her, in your opinion, to conduct a fair interview with Alex as she would any other applicant?" Tommy asked.

"Yes. She is a professional to the core. I cross-examined her as if she were a witness to determine if she has a bias for the Catholic Church. I don't believe she does. I believe she'll call it as she sees it," Willis answered.

"Okay, Silk, get with Alex and set up an interview with Dr. Turner. Let them both know that whatever the opinion of Dr. Turner turns out to be, it'll be presented at trial. That's my deal with Monsignor Renzulli."

"That's very risky, Tommy," Willis said.

"Maybe so, maybe not. If Alex is who she says she is and believes she is, then she should be deemed a capable applicant for the seminary. If she isn't capable, then she wouldn't be admitted even if she were a male. The time to find that out is now. An interview like this is as much a qualification to be accepted to the seminary for the church as the qualification of gender," Tommy replied.

"I still think that is risky," Willis said.

"There are only two answers. She is either qualified, or she's not. Joe Bob would take fifty-fifty anytime," Tommy said.

CHAPTER TWENTY-FIVE

After his meeting with Tommy O'Reilly, Monsignor Renzulli talked to Archbishop Sierra's assistant and requested an appointment with Archbishop Sierra at the earliest convenience of His Eminence. Later that afternoon, Sierra's assistant called Renzulli and said the archbishop was free to speak to the monsignor if the monsignor was available. Monsignor Renzulli went to Archbishop Sierra's office and was led in.

"Your Eminence," Monsignor Renzulli said, "I wish to talk to you about the lawsuit."

"Yes, Monsignor, I will always try to be at your disposal." he said gracefully. Jorge Sierra was not an imposing man. He was of medium height with a rotund frame, and his complexion was swarthy, befitting his Hispanic heritage. His face was capped by head of thinning gray hair combed straight back, and he looked like the grandfather everybody wished they had.

"I met with the plaintiff's attorney, Tommy O'Reilly," Monsignor Renzulli answered.

"What is your impression of the man?" Archbishop Sierra asked pleasingly.

"He's very much like how he is described in the investigation report I gave you. He's very opinionated and, in my opinion, of marginal intelligence. Some of his ideas and his interpretation of the Scriptures are ridiculous." Monsignor Renzulli then explained O'Reilly's opinion of the seventh commandment and papal infallibility.

"He does sound a bit off-center," Archbishop Sierra said quietly. "What do we need to discuss?"

"Mr. O'Reilly has contacted and has interviewed a number of theologians and scholars who are willing to testify that the church's foundation for a male-only priesthood is flawed and not based on sound theology. In other words, the reason the church has for the discrimination of women would not satisfy the legal definition of 'justifiable cause' under the law," Monsignor Renzulli answered.

"I'm not surprised. The church has always been under siege since the time of our Lord, and there always will be people who will attack it. But this is an issue that is so clear to me that I'm surprised there's even one reputable theologian who could scholarly justify the inclusion of a female to be a priest," Archbishop Sierra said.

Monsignor Renzulli replied, "I agree with you, but to counter his experts, we would need to put on the same number or more experts to present our position. The problem is that if we lose our motion and have to go to trial, a trial like this could take weeks, or even months. Judge Bateman's docket and calendar is so extended, we may not get a trial setting for two years at least."

"That might not be so bad," Archbishop Sierra said thoughtfully. "The more time it takes, the more likely the publicity will die down, and that will be a good thing."

"It may not be a good thing at all, Your Eminence," replied Renzulli. "I'm worried about copycat lawsuits. This is the first time ever a case of this nature has been brought against the church. If we have a quick hearing on the motion and we win, this will be over and done. If not, and we have to go to trial, we want a trial setting as quick as possible. If this drags on, others might think we're in a vulnerable position and might file in other jurisdictions. We would find ourselves defending on all fronts. The more cases filed, the more the odds are lessened in our favor. I believe it's in our best interests to have this matter resolved quickly."

"What do you suggest?" asked Archbishop Sierra.

"Tommy O'Reilly offered a deal because he wants a quick trial as well. I think it's because he's impatient and aggressive by nature. And second, he doesn't want his client hanging in the air for a year or two. He agreed to put on two witnesses only, Aleksandra Kowalski and one of the psychiatrists or psychologists who interview applicants for the seminary on behalf of the archdiocese. He or she will interview Ms. Kowalski and render an opinion on the capability of Ms. Kowalski for the seminary irrespective of gender," Monsignor Renzulli said.

"Why would he suggest that?" Archbishop Sierra asked.

"O'Reilly knows that the basic qualifications for entrance to the seminary are that a person has to be an unmarried male baptized in the Catholic religion. He also knows those qualifications alone will not gain an applicant entrance to the seminary. He knows that an applicant must take and successfully pass a psychological review and exam. He wants to make sure that if he's successful in his action on the gender issue, the review and exam will not be a detriment to his client gaining entrance to the seminary. He's confident she'll pass," Monsignor Renzulli answered.

"Who picks the examiner?" the archbishop asked.

"He will," Renzulli answered.

"We use five different examiners, and I know them all quite well," Archbishop Sierra responded. "They're all very professional and will give an objective interview to Ms. Kowalski. Whatever their opinion, they will tell the truth. What do we have to do in return?"

"We only put on one witness: just you, Your Eminence. On direct examination and in answers to my questions, you will tell and explain the Catholic Church's position for the male-only priesthood. After that he will cross-examine you and try to impeach you, and by that I mean try to punch holes in your testimony. However, he will be in your area of expertise and asking questions within your knowledge. Are you comfortable with that?" Monsignor Renzulli asked.

Archbishop Sierra thought a minute and then said quietly, "Yes, I am. I'm very confident in our position and therefore in my ability to support it. After all, how bad can it be? I have God on my side."

"Well, Your Eminence, that's the deal I made. Under the circumstances, I think it is an excellent deal for us."

"Then let's pray, Monsignor. We'll pray for the guidance of Judge Bateman so that he will sustain our motion, and if not, and a trial is necessary, we'll pray that the truth will win out."

And there in the office of Bishop Cardinal Sierra, the bishop of the Archdiocese of Galveston-Houston, two men bowed their heads and folded their hands and prayed silently to the God that they knew they represented on earth. They prayed that he would take care of and bestow his blessings upon his one true church.

CHAPTER TWENTY-SIX

John Bateman had entered his chambers, taken off his robes, and closeted them. He sat down at his desk and tried to calm himself. Those idiotic federal sentencing guidelines had infuriated him again. In order to correct a large disparity between jurisdictions in the sentencing of criminals, Congress had passed legislation to create the guidelines. Originally mandatory in nature, the US Supreme Court had ruled they were only advisory. Even so, if a trial judge strayed from the guidelines, the appellate court would likely overrule, and John Bateman did not like being reversed. He had just sentenced a drug dealer to three years in prison because of the guidelines. Three years only! In John Bateman's opinion, drugs were undermining the whole fabric of the United States, and drug suppliers were destroying the country much as any terrorist would do. If he could classify drug dealers as terrorists, he could have given thirty years or more instead of three; but it wasn't an option because being overruled wasn't an option.

He then looked at the case file on the top of his desk. It was the Kowalski file, and he had read and reread the briefs. Both of his staff attorneys had researched it independently. This was a close one, almost too close to call. He had been back and forth on the question, and he kept coming back and trying to second-guess the appellate court and what they would think. He didn't want to be reversed on whatever decision he ultimately made.

Stop it! he thought. *You're a federal judge for a reason. Make a decision not based upon what others might think, but what you think is right!*

He knew procrastination would only make things worse in this high-profile case. He needed to just make a decision, do whatever was right, not only for the parties, but also for those in the country who would be affected by the decision as a whole.

He picked up his telephone and called his clerk. He said, "The parties in the Kowalski litigation have requested an immediate hearing on the defendants' motion for summary judgment. I wish to get it set up for hearing as soon as possible. How soon can we have a special setting for a one-hour hearing?"

His clerk studied the docket for a moment then replied, "You have a trial setting this Friday starting at nine a.m. You could delay that and start jury selection one hour later and hear the motion at nine a.m."

"Okay, set it for that date and time and so advise both parties. Tell them they will have twenty minutes each for oral argument, and I'll put them on the clock," Judge Bateman instructed. He already felt better. The federal sentencing guidelines he could not do anything about; the biggest media case in the country? That he could do something about.

CHAPTER TWENTY-SEVEN

When Manuel pulled up to the courthouse on Friday morning at eight a.m., there were a number of news trucks with their antennae parked on the street. In front of the courthouse there were news reporters and cameramen standing two deep. Tommy surmised that the docket setting had been made known and the news people were there in anticipation of the arrival of the lawyers in Tommy's lawsuit. Tommy thought that this would be the most attended docket hearing in Harris County in a long while, and he knew that it would be an ordeal getting through the crush of people and the security lines inside the courthouse. He knew he would be at a standstill enough times that he would be bombarded with questions he didn't want to answer. He needed a diversion of some kind, and he had an idea.

"Manny, please loan me your iPod and headphones," Tommy asked.

"Sure thing, Mr. O'Reilly, but what for?" Manuel answered.

"I'm going to wear them in. Show me how to adjust the volume. I will want it loud enough that I'm not aware of the voices around me," Tommy said.

"You may not like my music," Manuel said.

"It doesn't matter. Just show me how to use the iPod," Tommy answered. Manuel showed him the controls, and after Tommy was familiar with the operation of the iPod, he put on the headphones and adjusted the volume. The music was Mexican salsa, and it was actually kind of nice. He was glad Manny wasn't into heavy metal or rap music. He stepped out of the car and adjusted the volume higher.

He said to Manuel, "This stuff is cool," and smiled. Manuel said something back to him, but he couldn't hear him at all, and Tommy was glad his idea was working. But Manuel's smile told Tommy he had liked what Tommy had said.

Tommy turned and started through the news people and was glad he could only hear the Latin beat. He did resist the urge to bob his head to the beat of the music; it probably wouldn't look good on the evening news. He walked ahead with a smile on his face and oblivious to anything but his destination ahead. When he reached the security line, he had to take them off and pass them through x-ray. Then he could hear questions shouted at him: "What'll you do if you lose?" and "Where's Aleksandra Kowalski? When can we interview her?" One person had the audacity to ask, "Is your hair color natural?" When he exited security, he put the headphones back on and went through another wave of reporters. When he entered the courtroom, the decorum changed remarkably. He took his headphones off and turned off the iPod, and it was quiet, as all courtrooms are required to be. The courtroom also had reporters seated, but they knew better than to yell questions. Instead they were here to record the "show." Tommy noticed no cameras were in the courtroom and thought Judge Bateman had prohibited them, which was normal procedure.

He took his seat at the plaintiff's table and looked over at the defendants' table. Monsignor Renzulli was there but dressed in the black suit of a priest with a white Roman collar and none of the purple designating the rank of monsignor. Seated next to him was another priest, similarly attired, whom Tommy assumed to be Father Murray, whom Betty had mentioned. Also seated at the table were two lawyers in civilian attire, a man and a woman, whom Tommy assumed to be local counsel. Tommy nodded to Monsignor Renzulli, and he nodded back.

At nine a.m. the bailiff announced, "All rise," and Judge Bateman entered the room and climbed the steps to his bench.

Judge Bateman said, "We're here in the matter of Aleksandra Kowalski versus the Archdiocese of Galveston-Houston and Bishop Cardinal Jorge Sierra. On the docket this morning is a hearing on the motion for summary judgment duly filed by the defendants. Is the counsel for the plaintiff present and ready?"

"We are, Your Honor," Tommy stood and said.

"Is counsel for the defendants present and ready?"

"We are, Your Honor," Monsignor Renzulli likewise answered.

"The court has received the motion and brief in support thereof from the defendants and the response and a brief in support thereof from the plaintiff," Judge Bateman said. "The court will allow twenty minutes of oral argument from each side. Monsignor, since it's your motion, you're up and on the clock."

CHAPTER TWENTY-EIGHT

Monsignor Renzulli stood up at the table for the defendants. Judge Bateman required oral arguments to be presented at the table and not at a lectern. He said, "Your Honor, I'll be brief since our position is stated in our motion and legal brief, and I'm sure Your Honor has read it."

"Thank you, Monsignor Renzulli, for not repeating your brief word for word, and yes, I have read it. Despite some opinions to the contrary among the legal community here in Houston, I do read briefs and understand them," Judge Bateman said. There was twitter and chuckling in the courtroom and Tommy knew that even with the lack of microphones the press would be able to hear Judge Bateman and the lawyers quite well.

Monsignor Renzulli started out quite simply. "Your Honor, our position is that the plaintiff is attempting to insert the government into the defendants' ecclesiastical rules, which has no precedent in American law."

Before he could continue, Judge Bateman interrupted, "Excuse me, Monsignor Renzulli, are you suggesting that because a certain set of facts has never been reviewed before by a court that the court has no power to review those facts as they pertain to existing law?"

"No, Your Honor," Monsignor Renzulli answered. "What I'm suggesting is that this set of facts, this cause of action, has not been reviewed before because it's so clear that no court has jurisdiction over the ecclesiastical rules of any church, as it is clearly prohibited by the First Amendment. No action of this kind would have been initiated by anyone with a fundamental knowledge of US constitutional law. Under the First Amendment, it's clear that the state, or a court on its behalf, may not intrude into the internal activities of a religious association or church."

"Monsignor Renzulli, my staff attorneys have researched what are commonly known as the sex scandal cases against the Catholic Church. A large number of courts have ruled they have jurisdiction over those activities, despite similar First Amendment arguments to the contrary. What is the difference here?" Judge Bateman asked.

"Your Honor, those cases involve pedophilia by a very small number of priests. The church became involved in litigation as a result of activities by certain bishops of the church after they discovered pedophilia by one or more priests. Although well-meaning by the bishops involved those activities were not official dogma or teaching of the Catholic Church," Monsignor Renzulli answered.

"So is it your position that the court has legal jurisdiction over unofficial activities of your church, but not over official activities of your church? If an unofficial activity is against the law and the court has jurisdiction, why wouldn't a court likewise have jurisdiction when an official activity is allegedly against the law?" Judge Bateman asked.

"The fundamental difference is that those unofficial activities were not an essential part of the religion of the Catholic Church. The cases you mention were based upon the alleged negligence of certain bishops and their actions after they discovered the pedophilia and how they handled the situation. The activities involved in those cases were not part of the religious doctrine of the Catholic Church, and therefore the guarantee of the freedom of religion does not apply to activities that are not part of the religious doctrine. What is at stake here is a fundamental and basic tenet of the Catholic religion and precisely that which the First Amendment guarantees the people of this country to believe and practice," Monsignor Renzulli argued.

Judge Bateman responded, "That is your argument even if the protection of that freedom under the First Amendment would cause the infringement of the rights of the plaintiff, who also has equal protection of the law to her rights?"

"Your Honor," Monsignor Renzulli answered, "enforcing her rights would result in the infringement of the Catholic Church's rights under the Constitution. Her rights arise out of legislation, and I submit that whenever an enacted law is in conflict with the Constitution, the Constitution is controlling, and that legislation is unconstitutional."

"Then is it your opinion that the Civil Rights Act is unconstitutional?" Judge Bateman asked.

"No, Your Honor, not the act. But the application of the act under the facts in this instance would be," Monsignor Renzulli answered.

"Do you have anything else, Monsignor?" Judge Bateman asked.

"No, Your Honor," Renzulli said.

Turning to Tommy, Judge Bateman said, "Mr. O'Reilly, it's your turn, and you are now on the clock."

"Your Honor, I will also be brief," Tommy started. "What we have here, Your Honor is a well-settled law that states that no one, and I emphasize no one, can discriminate against a woman solely because of her gender without justifiable reason. There is no question at all that the Catholic Church is discriminating against women by allowing only, and I quote, 'unmarried males who have been baptized in the Catholic Church' to a Catholic seminary. That is discrimination on its face.

"Do they have justifiable reason for that? The defendants claim that the First Amendment prohibits an examination of that issue. We vehemently disagree. Say, for example, a church as a basic tenet of its religion and as an official activity practiced human sacrifice. Could anyone reasonably say that this court could not review that practice under United States law?"

Before Tommy could continue, Judge Bateman interrupted and asked, "Mr. O'Reilly, human sacrifice would be the murder of another human being and would be a felonious crime. Are you suggesting that the Catholic Church is undertaking criminal activities in not allowing your client admission to their seminary?"

"No, Your Honor, I'm not suggesting that what they're doing is criminal. But what I am saying is that what they're doing is, on its face, is a violation of civil law. A law is a law. Is a civil law less important than a criminal law? I suggest that all laws are important. Federal courts have assumed jurisdiction over the Catholic Church in the violation of civil law in the cases which Your Honor previously mentioned. There is no difference here. This court clearly has jurisdiction over this matter. The defendants should be required to prove that their treatment of women is not discriminatory under the law. They should be required to prove they have justifiable cause to discriminate. The First Amendment does not protect them from this obligation," Tommy finished.

"Are you finished, Mr. O'Reilly?" Judge Bateman asked.

"Just one more point, Your Honor. I believe it's important to look at what the framers of the Constitution had in mind when they took pen in hand and wrote the First Amendment. They had just successfully won their independence from England, a country which at the time required all citizens to belong to the Church of England. The framers wanted all citizens to have the right to practice the religion of their choice, not to have a single religion dictated by the state. That's it.

"It goes without saying that those men did not intend that constitutional right to protect *illegal* activity. It was to protect *legitimate* activity. To do otherwise would be, in my opinion, a violation of due process. The defendants should be required to explain the reasons for their actions to a judge and jury, who would then make a determination whether those actions are legitimate activity are not. Now, Your Honor. I'm finished," Tommy said.

"Do you have any rebuttal, Monsignor?" Judge Bateman asked.

"Yes, Your Honor," Monsignor Renzulli said as he stood up at his table. "Plaintiff's counsel has raised the intent of those who drafted the Constitution and has suggested that it was not intended to protect illegal activity. I will agree, as I'm sure most people would with that statement. But let's look at the activity in question here. The Catholic Church was a predominant religion at the time the Constitution was drafted, and the male-only priesthood was a well-known fact. If they did not intend the First Amendment to protect an existing and well-known activity of any religion prevalent at the time, whether it was Quaker, Presbyterian, Lutheran, or Catholic, they would have made an exception. Obviously they didn't.

"I think it's important to also note that of the ten amendments in the Bill of Rights, this is the first one. It only seems logical that what they felt was most important would be listed first. This amendment has to supersede any subsequent legislation. *Freedom* means just that Your Honor. The unfettered right to do as one wishes without *any* restrictions.

Now, Your Honor, I'm also finished," Monsignor Renzulli said.

"Any counter rebuttal, Mr. O'Reilly?"

"No, Your Honor."

"Well, in that case, since we're finished with the oral arguments, the court is ready to rule on the motion," Judge Bateman said, and the courtroom abruptly became eerily quiet.

CHAPTER TWENTY-NINE

Judge Bateman began, "Our forefathers drafted some of the most poignant language in human history when they said 'All men are created equal.' Unfortunately, when they coined those words, they didn't mean men of color, because most of the signatories were slave owners themselves. Therefore, when courts centuries later looked at the purpose of those words in an attempt to define whether it applied to issues before them, any court bound by the signatories' purpose or intent could not apply it to men of color.

"At one time, a judge like me, who is long dead now, had the opportunity to review those words in light of the times when he sat on the bench, and not in light of the times in which the words were drafted. Although the original purpose was *not* to include black men as being equal to and to be afforded the same rights as white men, he nevertheless overturned the original intent and took the step to interpret those words to include *all* men of color. He set a precedent that was followed by other courts, which led to legislation that specifically included all men of color, the Civil Rights Act of 1964. That legislation also accomplished something that our forefathers also did not intend: it included women as well. Women in this country at the time of the

Constitution could not vote, own land, obtain a divorce, sign a legal document, or be educated beyond elementary school. They obviously were not intended to have the same rights as men by the framers of the Constitution. But today, all men and women of whatever color or creed have the same rights under the laws of this country. That is very clear.

"Monsignor Renzulli has argued this court has no jurisdiction over the defendants in this case, since their right to practice their religion under the First Amendment prohibits *any* interference by the government in that freedom. However, other courts have found jurisdiction over this same church when the activities of their church violated the laws of this country. The defendants argue that this is different, in that those activities were not officially sanctioned, nor were they part of the doctrine of their church.

"However, the defendants do not deny but readily admit they only allow men to qualify for the seminary, and I have to assume they believe they have justifiable cause to do so.

"The plaintiff has argued forcibly in her brief that a seminary is an institution of higher learning and has cited a number of cases where courts have ruled to allow women into institutions of higher learning when, prior to the ruling, those institutions were restricted to males. This court does take notice that none of those particular cases involves the First Amendment rights to freedom of religion. The plaintiff has also argued forcibly that the rights of one person should not be protected when that protection creates undue harm under the law to the legal rights of another. However, the defendants have argued that the protection of the rights of the plaintiff creates undue harm to their own legal rights, and their rights under the Constitution supersede her rights under legislation.

"In summary, this court is being asked to balance the conflicting legal rights of the parties involved in this lawsuit and determine which way the scales of justice tilts. To begin with, this court is persuaded that other courts have taken jurisdiction over the activities of the church involved in this case. This court is also persuaded that there is a basic fact question here over the activities of this church in this action. Do the defendants have justifiable cause to exclude women from the seminary which is an institution of higher learning? Since there is ample precedent to assume jurisdiction over the defendants and a fact question exists, I hereby overrule the motion for summary judgment and am prepared to set this cause for a trial setting," Judge Bateman finished.

Bingo, Tommy thought. He would take fifty-fifty any time!

There was an enormous outpouring of noise in the back of the courtroom, and Tommy heard the sounds of people leaving, no doubt the first wave of news people to get on camera and report the latest breaking events. He also had no doubt that they had left others behind to report on the rest of the proceeding.

Monsignor Renzulli immediately stood up and said, "Your Honor, we take exception to your ruling as a matter of law."

"Exception duly noted, Monsignor Renzulli," Judge Bateman replied.

"We also move for a stay in these proceedings so that we may file an appeal to the United States appellate court. If the appellate court should find in our favor, then this court and both parties would save the costs and time to try this case," Monsignor Renzulli argued.

"Motion to stay proceedings overruled, exception also noted," Judge Bateman said. He then turned to Tommy and said, "Mr. O'Reilly, you have requested a jury trial to determine whether justifiable cause exists on the part of the defendants, depending upon the testimony given at trial. Is that correct?"

"Yes, Your Honor," Tommy replied.

"You also recognize that this court will have the right to determine whether a mandatory injunction is justified, even if the jury determines that the defendants are not operating in a justified manner?" Judge Bateman asked.

"Yes, Your Honor," Tommy responded.

"What is your request, Mr. O'Reilly, regarding the size of the jury? Do you want a six-person or twelve-person jury?" Judge Bateman asked.

Tommy was quiet for a moment. He and Silk had discussed this at great length. Judge Bateman had the right to grant his request for a jury trial or not. If he did not grant the request, the question of justifiable reason of the defendants' actions would be solely Judge Bateman's to determine. He would also have the sole discretion to determine whether an injunction was in order. It was a lot of power in the hands of one person, and that is why Tommy had asked for a jury.

A jury could either be six or twelve jurors under the rules of this court. Tommy could request one or the other, but again Judge Bateman had full discretion on the size of the jury. On a twelve-person jury, the odds were more favorable to having women as jurors, which Silk felt would be more favorable to their case. On the other hand, twelve jurors would also increase the odds of more Catholics being on the jury, which would not favor their case. In either event, the court rules required a unanimous verdict of the jury. He and Silk had made a decision.

"Your Honor, the plaintiff requests a six-person jury." Tommy answered.

"Is there any specific reason you have requested six jurors and not twelve?" Judge Bateman asked.

Tommy thought, *Yes, there's less chance for Catholics, and we might still get a woman or two*, but said instead, "Yes, Your Honor. A smaller jury will require less time for jury selection and shorten the time needed on your docket, Your Honor."

After a moment or two of thought, Judge Bateman said "The court grants the plaintiff's request for a six-person jury. Now let's talk about a trial setting. Neither party has requested discovery, which is highly unusual. Is that still the position of the parties?"

"Yes, Your Honor," Tommy said.

"Yes, Your Honor," Monsignor Renzulli said.

"How many witnesses do you plan to call, Mr. O'Reilly?" Judge Bateman asked.

"Your Honor, I have made an agreement with Monsignor Renzulli. I will call two witnesses, and he will call one witness. That's it."

Judge Bateman looked somewhat stunned. In all of his years on the bench, this was a first. He asked, "What is your estimate of time of trial, Mr. O'Reilly?"

Tommy answered, "Two days."

"Monsignor Renzulli?"

"The same, Your Honor."

Judge Bateman turned to his law clerk and asked, "When can we have trial setting for a two-day duration?"

Dick Cole replied, "Your Honor, next week you had a trial set for four days beginning on Tuesday, but yesterday the parties notified the court that it had been settled. We could do it then if Your Honor would like to do so."

"Well in that case, trial is set for nine a.m. next Tuesday. Are there any questions?"

There were none, and then Judge Bateman ordered a ten-minute recess before starting the rest of his business for the day.

CHAPTER THIRTY

Michael stood up and left the courtroom. *This was horrible,* he thought. *That idiotic judge kept referring to the Catholic Church in a demeaning way. Bateman had a condescending way, and he seemed to have a total lack of respect for the teaching of the church. Who did he think he was, anyway, to overrule Monsignor Renzulli's motion? It was well thought out and well argued. Now six people who will probably know nothing of the faith will decide if a basic tenet of the church is justifiable? How ridiculous!*

He felt in his gut that the time to take action was getting close, but not yet! He would attend the trial and see how that went, and then see if God would call him to action. He had obtained all of the materials he needed, and everything was in place. He silently hoped he would be needed, and the thought stirred him.

CHAPTER THIRTY-THREE

Tuesday, the day of the trial, had arrived, and Manuel let Tommy, Silk, Alex, and Dr. Turner off at the back of the federal building. Judge Bateman had arranged for both of the parties, their counsel, and witnesses to use the private entrance that the judges and other employees used. Several days ago Tommy had interviewed Dr. Turner, and she advised that she had given the same psychological exam that she gave all applicants to the seminary. Alex had passed with flying colors, which, although not a surprise was a relief. Tommy had spent a morning with Dr. Turner to go over her report and the questions Tommy would ask her about the report. Tommy and Alex had also spent two days going over her direct testimony and then a practice cross-examination with questions that Tommy and Silk thought might be asked by Monsignor Renzulli. He thought she was as prepared as she could be.

They went into Judge Bateman's courtroom and took their places at the plaintiff's table, except for Dr. Turner, who took a seat in the pew right behind their table. This was the first time the press had seen Aleksandra Kowalski, except for yearbook pictures that some news hounds had dug up. She was a lady now, and not a high school or college student, and Tommy could hear a murmuring of voices behind him. He had no doubt that since cameras were prohibited, there were artists in the courtroom drawing a likeness of Alex for use by their various outlets. He looked over to the defendants' table, and the same people were there as were at the hearing except for one addition; Archbishop Jorge Sierra was there with the others dressed in a black suit with a white Roman collar, not the excessive trappings of an archbishop. Tommy thought he would have him dressed the same way.

At nine a.m., again, everyone stood when the bailiff intoned the "all rise" and then sat down when instructed. Before they could start their case, Judge Bateman had to deal with the myriad of criminal matters whose priority invariably consumed the docket of any federal judge. At ten thirty the court was finally ready for the trial that everybody was in attendance for except for the hapless criminal defendants, their attorneys, and the United States attorneys.

The bailiff stood and intoned, "This honorable court is now in session on the matter of Aleksandra Kowalski versus the Archdiocese of Galveston-Houston and Bishop Cardinal Jorge Sierra, Judge John Bateman presiding."

Judge Bateman looked at his bailiff and said, "Bailiff, will you please escort the jury panel in and have them seated by number?"

The bailiff said, "Yes, Your Honor," and left the courtroom and returned minutes later with forty people who would make up the jury panel. A questionnaire had been sent to all prospective jurors who had been subpoenaed for that week. The forty who made up the panel had been picked at random. Both counsel received copies of the questionnaire with the responses submitted by each of the members of the jury panel.

Other than the usual questions of name, occupation, address, and their particular history with lawsuits, included was an additional question that Tommy had requested, which Monsignor Renzulli had not objected to, and Judge Bateman had put in. It simply asked, "Are you a practicing Catholic? Yes or no." Sixteen of the forty people on the jury panel had answered yes. The jury panel had been numbered one through forty, and the numbers corresponded to their names. Since jurors were selected in numerical order of those left after challenges, the first fifteen were very important to Tommy and Monsignor Renzulli. Both he and Monsignor Renzulli had three preemptory challenges that they could use to excuse any three in the fifteen for any reason, which would leave nine remaining. They were also unlimited challenges for cause, which they could use on a juror whose answers to questions showed a bias for one side or the other.

Judge Bateman, however, would have to agree with the challenge for cause. Assuming both Tommy and Monsignor Renzulli would use their preemptory objections and there were no exceptions for cause, with nine left, the first six would serve on the jury, and the other three would serve as alternates if Judge Bateman desired. If any of the nine were excused, then number ten would be seated and so on down the line. At the request of the judge, the bailiffs swore in the forty prospective jurors.

The jury listened intently as Judge Bateman gave his instructions. "You're being asked to sit on the case of Aleksandra Kowalski versus the Archdiocese of Galveston-Houston and Bishop Cardinal Jorge Sierra. I will ask you a series of questions first, and then the attorneys will ask you a series of questions under what is known as *voir dire*. The purpose of these questions is to elicit your answers under oath and determine whether you can be an impartial juror, listen to the testimony of all witnesses objectively, and render a fair and impartial decision. Does anybody have a question about the process?"

After a brief silence with no response, Judge Bateman continued, "Other than those of you are Catholic and would be part of the archdiocese, do any of you personally know Aleksandra Kowalski or Archbishop Jorge Sierra?"

Again, with no response from the jury, Judge Bateman probed further. "Do any one of you know either Thomas Patrick O'Reilly, counsel for the plaintiff, or Monsignor Renzulli, counsel for the defendants?" Two people raised their hands, and under questioning said that Mr. O'Reilly had represented close family members. After questioning by Judge Bateman they were excused, and Tommy knew that the panel had gone to thirty-eight.

Judge Bateman cautioned the jury further. "This case has received a great amount of notoriety. Have any of you, by way of news reports, or any other sources, formed an opinion about this case one way or the other? Remember, you are under oath." Eighteen people raised their hands, twelve of whom had answered the questionnaire as being Catholic. They were all excused by Judge Bateman without being asked their opinion. They were now down to twenty, Tommy thought, still enough for a quorum.

Clearing his throat, Judge Bateman continued, "Of the rest of you, how many have read newspaper accounts or watched TV news reports about this lawsuit?" Everyone raised their hands except the small man with a dark complexion, juror number fifteen. Tommy wondered where he had been the last month. *Maybe he's been with Leroy and Benjamin watching Dancing with the Stars.*

Judge Bateman continued, "Those of you who have raised your hands, will the news reports you have either read or heard influence your decision in any way in this case? If so, please raise your hand." No one did.

"You will hear sworn testimony from witnesses over the next two days, which could very well conflict with has been reported in news accounts. You will be sworn to ignore what you have heard on the news. Is there anyone who will have a difficult time doing this? If so, please raise your hand." Again, no one did.

Satisfied he had an impartial jury panel, Judge Bateman glanced at the clock and said, "We are close to the noon hour. We will recess for lunch, and you will go with the bailiff to the cafeteria in the basement. You are instructed to stay together and not to talk to anyone unless they are on the jury panel. You may talk among yourselves about anything you wish but *not* about this case. Is that clear?"

All in the panel nodded in the affirmative.

"For those of you who will be selected for the jury to hear testimony in this case, those will be your instructions until you are dismissed."

Again glancing at the clock, Judge Bateman continued, "Court will be adjourned until one thirty, at which time counsel will ask questions of their own as I discussed with you previously."

After lunch, once everyone was seated at their respective tables, Tommy began his *voir dire*. He mainly concentrated on the remaining Catholics, inquiring about their bias for or against a woman priest. In his *voir dire*, Monsignor Renzulli left the Catholics alone and concentrated on the women and their affiliations with pro-feminist groups. The questioning by both counsels took up most of the afternoon, with panel members being excused either peremptorily or for cause.

The first six in order of the remaining numbers included two women and four men, one of the men being Catholic. The final panel would have included two Catholics, except that Tommy had challenged one juror for cause when he asked if he had a problem going to Mass and Communion presided over by a woman priest.

When the juror answered, "I don't know. How can I call her Father?" it was a no-brainer. One of the final six jurors was the dark-skinned man who had not watched news reports of lawsuit, but had volunteered on questioning that he was of the Hindu religion.

Judge Bateman announced adjournment until the following morning at nine a.m. As Tommy and Willis were leaving the courtroom, Tommy asked, "Silk, what do Hindus believe in?"

"I don't even have a clue, Tommy. We didn't have any Hindus in the 'hood where I grew up." Then he chuckled and said, "The only dos in the 'hood were the ones on the brothers' heads."

"Silk, we need to find out what Hindus believe in and quick!"

CHAPTER THIRTY-TWO

On Wednesday, the next morning, Judge Bateman's court went into session promptly at nine a.m. As plaintiff, Tommy O'Reilly had the first opening argument. Tommy was brief and to the point. He said, "The evidence will clearly show that the plaintiff, Aleksandra Kowalski, is in every way but one an appropriate candidate to enter the seminary and study for the priesthood. The only qualification she lacks that the Catholic Church requires is the anatomy of a male. There will be no dispute about this. The only question of fact that you, the jury, will have is to determine whether the defendants have justifiable cause to discriminate against the female gender.

"The evidence will also show that the Catholic Church professes and teaches it is the first church established by Jesus Christ. The evidence will further show that the defendants will rely not on what Jesus Christ did, but what Jesus Christ did not do in order to justify their position of gender discrimination. Their position is Jesus Christ did not name women as apostles and therefore meant to exclude women forever from the Catholic clergy. There are a number of reasons why Jesus Christ acted as he did, other than to forever deny women to be priests, and the evidence will show this. If you believe the evidence, and I believe you will, then you will have no choice but to find for the plaintiff."

Monsignor Renzulli was equally brief and to the point. He said, "The evidence will show the defendants have a proper interpretation of the Scriptures on their side. It will further show that for two thousand years since the time of Christ, the Catholic Church has been consistent in the interpretation of the Scriptures. It will also show that the Catholic Church is not discriminatory against women and that women are given special places of honor in the Catholic Church.

"The evidence will also show that the teaching of the male-only priesthood is, in the eyes of the church, the will of God. It follows the example of Jesus Christ. The church could not change this doctrine even if it wanted to. The preponderance of the evidence will show that the defendants do not discriminate against women by the doctrine of the male-only priesthood. It's the only logical result based upon the church's religious teaching, and as such, the only choice you will have is to find for the defendants."

Judge Bateman then asked Tommy to call his first witness.

"Your Honor, we call Aleksandra Kowalski to the stand," Tommy said.

A slight murmur resonated from the back of the court as Aleksandra Kowalski left the plaintiff's table and walked to the witness stand. After she had been sworn in and after Tommy had elicited her name, background information, parents' address, purposely leaving out the address of the nunnery where she currently lived, he asked, "Did you apply to the Archdiocese of Galveston-Houston to attend the seminary in its jurisdiction?"

"Yes, Mr. O'Reilly, I did."

"Did they accept your application?" Tommy asked.

"No, Mr. O'Reilly, they did not."

"Did they tell you why they did not accept your application?"

"I was told I did not meet the basic qualifications for an applicant to the seminary," Alex answered.

"What are the basic qualifications for being an applicant to the seminary?" Tommy asked.

"An applicant must be a non-married male baptized in the Catholic Church," Alex replied.

"What is your gender, Miss Kowalski?" Tommy asked.

"I'm of the female gender."

"Miss Kowalski, are you married, or have you ever been married?"

"No, Mr. O'Reilly, I'm not married, nor have I ever been married," Aleksandra said firmly.

"Are you a Catholic baptized in the Catholic Church?" Tommy asked.

"Yes, Mr. O'Reilly, I'm a baptized Catholic."

"So if I understand you correctly, you fulfill the qualifications of being unmarried and baptized in the Catholic Church. Is that correct?"

"Yes, Mr. O'Reilly."

"Therefore, the only reason your application to attend the seminary was denied is because you are not a male. Is that correct?"

Monsignor Renzulli stood and exclaimed, "Objection, Your Honor, the question calls for a conclusion of the witness that is not within her scope of knowledge."

"Sustained," Judge Bateman said.

Tommy recovered quickly. "Are there any other qualifications to be a qualified applicant to the seminary other than what you had previously stated?" Tommy asked Alex.

"No, Mr. O'Reilly."

"Are you married or have you ever been married?" Tommy asked.

"Objection, Your Honor, question has been asked and answered," Monsignor Renzulli stated.

"Sustained," Judge Bateman said.

Tommy let it go; the jury had gotten his point. Then he asked, "Ms. Kowalski, why do you want to be a priest?"

Aleksandra answered just as she had rehearsed with Tommy. Her voice was soft and feminine but full of conviction as she looked earnestly at the jury, as Tommy had taught her to do. "Don't look at me," he had said. "I'm not the one you're trying to convince. Look at the jury!"

"I want to be a priest because I believe it is my calling in life, and it's something I have felt since I was very young. When I was asked what I wanted to be when I grew up, as all children are, I would say a priest, and everyone would laugh and say 'You can't be a priest. You're a girl!' What difference does that make? I looked around at all the boys, and they could be priests, but I couldn't! I was smarter than they were, more caring than they were, and more committed to the Catholic Church than they were. As I grew older the calling became stronger, and I know I have the spirituality, the desire to help others, and the dedication to do God's work."

"How does the position of the church against women make you feel?" Tommy asked quietly.

"I feel very frustrated and abused as I sit here just because I don't have male genitalia! If I did, none of us would be here today. I could have a sex change operation, and the church would have to check the box on gender, but would that make me a better priest? Of course not!"

"Objection, Your Honor" Renzulli interrupted. "The witness is asking and answering her own questions!"

"Sustained," Judge Bateman said. Turning to Aleksandra, he continued, "Miss Kowalski, please limit your testimony to answering the questions which are asked of you."

"Yes, Your Honor. I'm sorry" Aleksandra said contritely.

Tommy recovered smoothly and said, "Let's get back to the gender requirement of the church. Is there any role for male genitalia in priestly functions that you know of?"

"No," she said, looking back at the jury. "In fact, all priests take a vow of celibacy, so the requirement of male genitalia makes no sense."

"You mentioned a calling. Do you know if God is calling you to the priesthood?" Tommy asked.

"Objection, Your Honor!" Monsignor Renzulli interrupted again. "She cannot possibly know what's in the mind of God. This is obviously calling for a conclusion outside the scope of knowledge of this witness," Monsignor Renzulli said.

"Sustained," Judge Bateman said.

Tommy thought Bateman was not giving him much leeway, but the last objection might bite Monsignor Renzulli in the butt later, and he made a quick note on his legal pad.

"Ms. Kowalski, let's talk about your feelings, which are something you do know about. Do you honestly *feel* that God is calling you to be a priest?" Tommy asked.

"Yes, Mr. O'Reilly. I truly feel that he's calling me to be a priest."

Willis had been watching the jury very carefully and noticed they had been dutifully listening to every word of Alex's testimony. Tommy had gotten everything in that they had wanted to, and the jury was engaged. They had shown gender discrimination, which is all they wanted to do. In the end, the verdict would come down to the justification of the defendants' actions, which was not anything Alex could testify about. Willis wrote a note to Tommy that said "pass."

Tommy looked at the note and then his notes and said, "Your Honor, we pass the witness."

Monsignor Renzulli immediately jumped up from his table. "Ms. Kowalski, if you are ordained as a Catholic priest, are you aware that you will take a vow to obey all teachings of the Catholic Church?

"Yes, Monsignor Renzulli, I'm aware of that vow."

"Are you aware the Catholic Church teaches that only males may be validly ordained as priests?"

"Yes, Monsignor, I'm aware of that doctrine."

"Do you believe in the doctrine concerning the gender of priests?" Renzulli asked.

"No, Monsignor, I do not."

"Then how can you in all good conscience take the vow to obey all teachings of the Catholic Church when you do not believe in the validity in one of the basic doctrines of the church?" Renzulli asked.

"Monsignor, I could in all good conscience take that vow," Aleksandra answered.

"Will you kindly please tell the jury how that can possibly be?" asked the Monsignor.

Looking at the jury she smiled and said, "If I'm ordained as a priest, the very fact that I'm ordained would necessarily mean that teaching is no longer taught. After all, I would be both a woman and an ordained priest. I could readily take a vow to obey all doctrines then validly taught by the church."

She noticed some of the jurors smiled back at her after her answer.

Renzulli changed subjects and asked, "Miss Kowalski, there has been a good bit of notoriety about your lawsuit, wouldn't you agree?"

"Yes, Monsignor."

"It might make one wonder how sincere you are about your vocation or whether you're seeking publicity."

"Objection!" Tommy shouted. "Counsel is not asking a question of the witness but is lecturing her."

"Sustained. Please confine your examinations to questions, Monsignor."

"You testified that you have had the calling to be a priest since you were a child, and you feel that this is a calling from God. Correct?"

"Yes."

When did you apply to the seminary?"

"I applied about a year ago."

"Ms. Kowalski, you testified you are thirty-three years of age. Ninety-nine per cent of all priests apply to the seminary in their twenties. Why did it take so long for you to apply to the seminary if you're really sincere about becoming a priest, or do your motives lie somewhere else?" Renzulli asked.

"I don't know. You'll have to ask God." There was laughter in the courtroom, and Judge Bateman had to bang his gavel and call for order.

Renzulli continued, "Unfortunately, God is not on the witness stand, Ms. Kowalski. You are. Again, why did it take you so long to apply to the seminary?"

"I don't know. It started about a year ago, and the more I prayed about it, the more I was convinced he was directing me to apply to the seminary so I could fulfill his desire for me to be a priest."

Monsignor Renzulli looked at her closely and asked, "Are you aware there are many Christian religions that would readily take someone who is as dedicated as you say you are to be a priest or a minister?"

"Yes, Monsignor, I'm aware of that."

"Then why did you not apply to one of those religious seminaries instead of filing a lawsuit against the Catholic Church to allow you entrance into the Catholic seminary?" Monsignor Renzulli asked.

"Because I'm a Catholic, and I wish to be a Catholic priest."

Monsignor Renzulli looked at his notes and said, "No further questions, Your Honor." He felt he had made a point that might be crucial to the outcome of this lawsuit.

"Any redirect examination, Mr. O'Reilly?" Judge Bateman inquired.

"No, Your Honor."

"The witness is excused. Call your next witness, Mr. O'Reilly," Judge Bateman said.

"The plaintiff calls Dr. Sylvia Turner," Tommy stated.

Dr. Turner was an attractive middle-aged woman with gray hair. She was small with a slight build, and with her horn-rimmed glasses, black suit, and white blouse, she looked exactly like what she was, a college professor. After initial questions about her name, address, and where she worked, Tommy spent fifteen minutes inquiring about her education, positions held and honors received, all of which were extensive. He concluded by requesting the court to acknowledge Dr. Turner as an expert in determining the qualifications of a candidate for the seminary. Monsignor Renzulli had no objection, since Dr. Turner worked for the archdiocese in the area of her expertise. Judge Bateman certified Dr. Turner as an expert.

"Dr. Turner, will you please describe the process by which you examine potential applicants to the seminary?" Tommy asked.

"Yes, Mr. O'Reilly," she answered. "To begin with, by the time we interview them, the candidates have been recommended by the priests and the pastor of the parish in which they live. Since priests know what it takes to be a priest, they are best able to assess whether a candidate has all of the outward attributes to be a priest. So our process is culling. We're looking for two qualities that may not be readily noticeable, the absence of pathology and the presence of good mental health. We try to do this in two ways, a face-to-face interview and by written examinations."

"Let's talk about the interview first. What questions do you ask?" Tommy queried.

Dr. Turner looked at the jury and said, "We ask about past sexual experiences such as, 'When was the last time you had sex?' Three years or more is the preferred answer. 'Last night' or 'last week' would be quite detrimental to the candidate. In addition we ask about masturbation fantasies, parental relationships, romantic relationships and the cause of those breakups, and alcohol consumption. Depending upon the answers to those questions, we might go deeper, particularly in the area of alcohol and sex. We might ask how they control their sexual desires, such as cold showers, long runs, etc. Our observations are as important as the answers to see if there is eye avoidance or other facial expressions that might indicate lying."

"Do you use a lie detector in your face-to-face interviews?" Tommy asked.

"No, we rely on our training."

"Very well. Please tell us about the other examinations," Tommy said.

Again looking at the jury, she said, "All candidates must take an HIV test, which is not administered by us, and a number of written examinations, which are. An example is the 567 question, Minnesota Multiphasic Personality Inventory, which screens for a number of things, including gender confusion, paranoia, and depression. These are very detailed examinations that reveal a lot about the candidate."

"Dr. Turner, did you perform the same tests on Aleksandra Kowalski that you use on all applicants to the seminary for the Archdiocese of Galveston-Houston?" Tommy asked, also looking at the jurors.

"Yes, I did," she said firmly.

"Based upon your interview and written examination of Aleksandra Kowalski, did you form an opinion about her fitness to be a candidate for the seminary?" Tommy asked.

"Yes, I did."

"What is that opinion, Dr. Turner?" Tommy asked.

"She tested admirably," Dr. Turner said forcefully. "If she had been of the right gender, there is no doubt in my mind that she would have been readily accepted to the seminary."

"No further questions, Your Honor. I pass the witness," Tommy said.

Monsignor Renzulli stood up and asked, "Dr. Turner, there seems to be a lot of subjectivity rather than objectivity in your process. Would you agree with that statement?"

"Yes, Monsignor, it's not a black-and-white process. It's hard to define what we do, but it's kind of like an 'I'll know it when I see it' type of thing," she answered directly.

"You're a woman. What is your opinion of whether a woman should be a priest?" Renzulli asked.

"I do not have one," she replied firmly.

"Really. None at all?" Renzulli countered.

"No. None at all," she answered.

"Dr. Turner, are you Catholic?"

"Yes I am."

"In your work, have you come across any studies that show only a very small percentage of practicing Catholics don't have an opinion on this issue?"

"No, I have not."

"So you would not be able to disagree with studies that indicate that most Catholic women are very opinionated about whether women should or should not be allowed to the priesthood."

"No."

Renzulli looked at her and smiled and said, "But you are one of the few women who don't care one way or the other, correct?"

"I don't know how small the minority is, but yes I don't care one way or the other."

"Surely in your work you have witnessed women who have been discriminated in society. Is that true?" Renzulli asked.

"Yes."

"Is the field in which you work dominated by men?"

"Mostly, but it is getting better."

"As a woman who has succeeded in a field dominated by men, you're telling this jury that there's not just a little part of you wanting the plaintiff to succeed in her quest to be a priest that might have influenced the subjective part of your process. Is that what you're saying?" asked Renzulli somewhat heatedly.

"Yes, that's what I'm saying," Dr. Turner matched the tone that was in Renzulli's voice. She continued, "Monsignor, the reason I have succeeded in a field dominated by men is that I am not biased by gender or anything else. I have done one thing and one thing only. I call 'em like I see 'em. That's what I'm telling this jury."

Monsignor Renzulli once again looked at his notes and said, "No further questions, Your Honor."

"Mr. O'Reilly, do you have any redirect?"

"No, Your Honor," Tommy answered.

Judge Bateman looked at the clock and announced, "We're coming up on the lunch hour. These proceedings will be adjourned until two o'clock. Court is dismissed until that time."

The bailiff said, "All rise," and Judge Bateman exited his courtroom, followed by everyone else in the room, including Michael.

CHAPTER THIRTY-THREE

After lunch and after the court had been called back into session, Judge Bateman said, "I believe that's all of your witnesses, Mr. O'Reilly, so, Monsignor Renzulli, you may now proceed."

Monsignor Renzulli called Bishop Cardinal Sierra to the stand. *Now the real action starts,* Tommy thought. Everything up to now had been establishing the record for what everyone knew: the only reason Aleksandra Kowalski was not accepted to the seminary was because of her gender. He didn't think that Renzulli had sufficiently impeached Dr. Turner's objectivity on her other qualifications. So other than gender, he had proven Aleksandra was an excellent candidate. Now it was time to see if the church could justify its actions.

After peremptory questions by Monsignor Renzulli about the archbishop's education, training and positions held in the church, which Tommy thought were indeed impressive, Renzulli began to get to the heart of the testimony.

"You stated you're the head of the Archdiocese of Galveston-Houston. Is that correct?" Monsignor Renzulli asked.

"Yes, that is correct," Bishop Sierra answered quietly.

"As bishop of an archdiocese, are you a cardinal of the Catholic Church?" Renzulli asked.

"Yes, I am," Bishop Sierra answered again.

"Is that the highest designation in the Catholic Church other than his Holy Father, the Pope?" Renzulli inquired.

"Yes, it is," Sierra answered humbly.

"Is that why you may be called either Archbishop Sierra or Bishop Cardinal Sierra?" Monsignor Renzulli asked.

"Yes," Sierra responded.

"Which title do you prefer?"

"Just 'bishop' is fine with me," Bishop Sierra said, smiling at the jury as they smiled back.

"As head of the Archdiocese of Galveston-Houston, are you the ultimate authority to approve or disapprove an applicant to the seminary in this archdiocese?" Monsignor Renzulli asked.

"Yes, I am."

"What are the basic qualifications for an applicant to be admitted to the seminary?"

Bishop Sierra responded, "The basic qualifications are that the candidate has to be an unmarried male baptized in the Roman Catholic Church."

"Why are unmarried women baptized in the Roman Catholic Church not qualified?" Renzulli asked.

"It has been the teaching of the Catholic Church since the time of Christ that all priests shall be of the male gender," Bishop Sierra answered forcefully.

"Is there a direct scriptural reference that is the foundation for this teaching?" Monsignor Renzulli asked.

"No."

"Then, Bishop Sierra, will you please explain to the jury the foundation of this doctrine?" Monsignor Renzulli asked.

"Yes, I will be glad to." Bishop Sierra then turned and looked directly at the jury and said, "First of all, Jesus chose only men to be his apostles. They were the rock upon which Jesus founded his church. The apostles were ordained by Jesus at his Last Supper as the first priests of the Catholic Church. Jesus had many women among his followers and could have easily chosen a woman to be among the apostles. The fact he did not appoint a woman is very significant and important. We follow the example that Jesus set two thousand years ago."

"Bishop Sierra, what were the social conditions of a woman in Palestine and Jerusalem at the time of Jesus?" Renzulli asked.

"The society in which Jesus lived was very much a male-dominated society. Women were considered little more than slaves. There was no equality at all among men and women at the time," Bishop Sierra answered.

"Perhaps the fact that Jesus did not appoint a woman as an apostle was because he was following the social norms of the times. Correct?" Monsignor Renzulli asked.

"No."

"Why is that not true, Bishop Sierra?" Renzulli asked.

Again looking at the jury, Bishop Sierra said, "Unlike the males of his time, Jesus treated women equally in all respects, which was a total break from the social customs of the times. He could have easily named a woman as an apostle and would have been totally consistent with his beliefs and actions. He was also establishing a new religion, one that was different from the Hebrew religion, which had only male rabbis. At the time there were many non-Hebrew religions that had women as priestesses. He could easily have named a woman as an apostle, and it wouldn't have been extraordinary for his new religion. It would also have been accepted by the disciples. The fact he did not do so is proof that he did not want to do so."

"You said 'first of all.' Does that mean there other reasons?"

"Yes."

"What are they?"

Again looking at the jury directly, Bishop Sierra responded, "Second of all, his example for selecting only men to the priesthood has been followed ever since his death and resurrection. The apostles, who knew Jesus better than anybody except for his mother, had an opportunity to name a woman to replace Judas. Judas was one of the original apostles who betrayed Jesus Christ and committed suicide as a result. The Scriptures name a number of women who were followers of Jesus and who would have been excellent candidates to be named as an apostle and therefore a priest.

"One of those women was his mother, Mary, whom the early church venerated as the mother of God and still does so today. The apostles knew her well and also knew the love for her that Jesus had. They chose not to pick the perfect person to replace Judas, and there is no evidence whatsoever she wished to be appointed. She knew Jesus better than anybody, and this suggests that she knew that her appointment as an apostle was not his will. After all Jesus could have appointed her in the first place and didn't. The will of Jesus Christ has been faithfully followed by the Catholic Church ever since."

Renzulli looked at the jury and saw they were paying rapt attention. He glanced back at Sierra and said, "You said, 'Second of all.' Again, are there other reasons than what you have provided so far?"

"Yes," Bishop Sierra said to the jury, "Jesus was God, and he could have easily been born a woman, but he chose to be a man. He constantly referred to his Father, who had also chosen to be recognized as the Father of the Hebrew religion in the Old Testament. But Jesus Christ as God became man, which Catholics call the Incarnation. God became man, not woman, and he took a very specific form of gender. Priests are the representatives of Jesus and the form of the human being he took on earth. A man can better represent Christ on earth than a woman, because Jesus was a man, and priests are also men."

Monsignor Renzulli lifted his notes, folded them, and said, "Thank you, Bishop Sierra, I have no further questions."

Monsignor Renzulli and Bishop Sierra had talked at length about his testimony and strategy. They had agreed that Bishop Sierra would state the church's position and the reasoning behind it and leave it at that. They had established a quite justifiable and defensible reason for the church's position. O'Reilly had no witnesses to refute Bishop Sierra's testimony, and it would be up to O'Reilly to try to punch holes in it on cross-examination. Since Bishop Sierra's knowledge of the church teachings and its foundation would be many times that of O'Reilly, they both felt confident that O'Reilly would have a difficult time in the cross-examination of Bishop Sierra. As he sat down, Monsignor Renzulli said a silent prayer that he had not underestimated O'Reilly.

"Your witness, Mr. O'Reilly," Judge Bateman said.

CHAPTER THIRTY-FOUR

"Bishop Sierra," Tommy began, "I believe you said there is no direct scriptural revelation that Jesus of Nazareth wanted to forever bar women from the priesthood and to reserve that honor to males only into perpetuity. Is that correct?"

"There is no direct order by Jesus in the Scriptures to reserve the priesthood for males only," Sierra answered.

"So your answer would be yes, correct?" Tommy said firmly.

"In the context in which I have just stated it, my answer will be yes," Sierra said back firmly.

Way to go, Renzulli thought. Don't let him put words in your mouth.

Tommy continued, "Without an explicit direction in the Scriptures, I believe your testimony is that the church relies upon what Jesus Christ didn't do but could have done in appointing males only as the twelve apostles. Is that correct?" Tommy asked.

"Mr. O'Reilly, as I testified previously, there are any number of scriptural references that indicate his opinion and will on a male-only priesthood, that example being just one of them."

"Why did Jesus appoint twelve apostles instead of two, ten, or twenty?" Tommy asked.

"The twelve apostles corresponded to the twelve tribes of Israel, which was in fulfillment of the Hebrew Scriptures," Bishop Sierra answered.

"Were any of the twelve tribes of Israel led by a woman at any time?" Tommy asked.

"Not that we are aware of," Bishop Sierra responded.

"So it would have made sense at the time in order to continue that tradition to have all males as the twelve apostles. Is that correct?" Tommy asked.

"I don't understand your question," Sierra said.

"Okay, I may put it another way. The number twelve for the apostles was selected intentionally to match the number of the tribes of Israel. Is that right?" Tommy asked.

"Yes, we think so. We don't know for sure, but that's what we understand."

"If Jesus, as you surmise, was following the tradition of the tribes of Israel, which had an all-male hierarchy, wouldn't it have made sense to continue the all-male hierarchy in the appointment of apostles?" Tommy asked again.

"Maybe," Sierra answered.

"He was starting a new religion different from but in fulfillment of the Hebrew religion, correct?"

"Yes."

"Wouldn't his new religion eventually have to break from the traditions of the Hebrew religion? Otherwise it would be the same religion, not a totally new one. Correct?" Tommy asked.

"Probably."

Tommy continued, "As his new religion developed and broke away from the traditions of the Hebrew religion, what he did at the outset and made sense at the beginning would no longer be required many, many years afterward. Is that correct?"

"I suppose so. But if the tradition or practice was also a fundamental part of his new religion, it would still be required such as reserving the priesthood to males," Sierra responded.

"Now, let's talk about some of the other characteristics the original apostles had besides being male," Tommy said. "Would you agree that they all probably wore beards, since that was one of the social norms of the time?"

"Yes."

"Did Jesus mean to forever exclude priests who were clean shaven?" Tommy asked.

"No, of course not. That was only an incidental characteristic that the apostles shared at the time," Bishop Sierra answered.

"Yes, Bishop Sierra that would be ridiculous. Wouldn't it? He probably would not even have had a choice to select someone who was clean shaven anyway, would he?" Tommy asked.

"Probably not," Sierra answered.

"As the social customs changed and beards were no longer in fashion, that characteristic would not be relevant at all, would it?" Tommy asked.

"It wasn't relevant in the first place. Beards were merely coincidental characteristics."

"I believe you also said that it was a social custom at the time not to put women in a position of leadership since they were treated only slightly above slaves. Is that correct?" Tommy asked.

Bishop Sierra adjusted himself in the witness chair and said, "Yes, I said that."

"The custom concerning the treatment of women as little more than slaves has also changed over time. Correct?" Tommy asked.

"It most certainly has," Sierra answered.

"In summary, we have two social customs at the time of Jesus that defined the apostles, both of which have changed over time. One you and the Catholic Church deem relevant and the other irrelevant to the qualifications of a priest today. Is that correct?" Tommy asked.

"Yes, a beard is merely incidental, and gender is fundamental," Bishop Sierra responded firmly.

"So you say," Tommy said. "Now let's talk about the other characteristics of the apostles. Most theologians believe all the apostles were probably married. If indeed that was the case, did that mean Jesus intended priests forever to be married?" Tommy asked.

"No."

"If he intended it, that would fly directly in the face of the doctrine of the Catholic Church requiring priests to be exactly the opposite, which is unmarried. Wouldn't it?" Tommy asked.

"Yes," Sierra responded.

"So the fact they were married was merely incidental and not fundamental?" Tommy asked.

Bishop Sierra sighed and said, "Yes, if in fact they were all married."

"All of the first apostles were also Jews, weren't they?" Tommy asked.

"Yes."

"There were a number of non-Jews or what were called Gentiles at the time among his followers. Is that true?" Tommy asked.

"Yes."

"Then he certainly could have appointed one or more Gentiles to be among the original apostles, is that correct?"

"Yes, he could have," Bishop Sierra answered.

"Does the fact he didn't appoint Gentiles to be among the original apostles mean that Gentiles were barred forever from the priesthood?" Tommy inquired.

"No."

Tommy looked directly at the jury and asked Sierra, "Why not, Bishop Sierra?"

Bishop Sierra responded, "The original church was comprised mostly of the Jewish race. As that church followed his command to 'go and teach all nations,' then Gentiles became an integral part of the church, and it was natural Gentile men would become ordained as priests."

"Since the original church was comprised of the Jewish race, it would have been very difficult to appoint a Gentile into a religious hierarchy like the twelve apostles. Is that not correct?" Tommy asked.

"Objection! Question calls for a conclusion of the witness," Monsignor Renzulli exclaimed.

"Your Honor," Tommy said, "the witness is an archbishop and cardinal in the Catholic Church. It is the second highest office in the church and certainly his scope of knowledge would include the reasons for the actions of Jesus Christ. He has already given an opinion in direct testimony about some of his activities."

After a moment of thought, Judge Bateman said, "Objection is overruled. Please answer the question, Bishop."

"Jesus could have done whatever he wanted and appointed whomever he wanted to be one of his apostles," Sierra said firmly.

"Yes, indeed. You have said that. He could have appointed a woman or a gentile to be an apostle despite the tremendous social pressures, which existed, but he didn't. Yet his example concerning the exclusion of Gentiles and women as one of the original priests is followed today by your church *only* with respect to women, correct?"

Bishop Sierra looked at Tommy and said, "Yes."

Tommy looked at his notes, at the jury, and then directly at Bishop Sierra, and said, "Bishop Sierra, I would like to summarize your testimony and make sure the jury and I understand it. Jesus appointed twelve apostles, and they all had common characteristics, such as the ones we have talked about and probably others, such as a common language and little or no education. As the church grew and social customs and mores changed, the church determined that all of those characteristics except one were merely incidental for the priesthood, but the male gender was fundamental. Why is the gender of the original apostles the only fundamental characteristic, while all the rest of the characteristics of the apostles were incidental? Aren't they all the result of the social customs of the times in which Jesus lived?"

"For the reasons I previously stated," Bishop Sierra answered.

"Do you not see the inconsistencies in your testimony?" Tommy asked pointedly.

Bishop Sierra looked directly back at Tommy and said, "No, I don't, not at all."

"Let's talk some more about what you have previously testified. You stated that women were little more than slaves, but Jesus treated women equally with men. Is that correct?"

"Yes."

"Now let's talk about slavery. Was slavery an accepted social custom of the times in which Jesus lived?" Tommy asked.

"Yes, it was readily accepted in Roman society."

"Could Jesus have appointed a slave as an apostle?" Tommy asked.

"He could have chosen anyone as I have said," Bishop Sierra answered.

"But he didn't appoint a slave, did he?" Tommy continued.

"No, he didn't."

"No, he didn't. In fact, he often used the relationship of master and slave in his parables to his disciples, didn't he?" Tommy asked.

"Yes."

"But he never spoke out against slavery in his parables or in his teachings, did he?" Tommy asked.

"Not that I am aware of," Bishop Sierra answered.

"Why do you suppose he didn't take a stand against slavery and speak out against it, as he did a number of other practices that he disagreed with at the time?" Tommy asked.

"I don't know. I've never really thought about it," Bishop Sierra answered.

"Could it be that slavery was so ingrained in the social norms of the time that if he had done so it would have been on the order of a tremendous social reform? Could it be that the times were not right for such a revolutionary idea and to do so would take the focus away from the religious reform he was trying to establish?" Tommy asked.

Bishop Sierra raised his eyebrows and said, "As I have said, I have never given it much thought."

"I asked you if it was possible," Tommy responded.

"Anything is possible, but not everything is probable." Bishop Sierra sneered.

"Was Jesus on earth to undertake a revolution and social upheaval?" Tommy asked.

"No."

"What about putting a woman in a position of leadership? Would the male-dominated society in which Jesus lived have rebelled against such a revolutionary social change so that the message he was trying to deliver about religious reform have lost focus? Is that also possible?" Tommy asked.

"No."

"But the truth is he didn't seek to abolish the entrenched custom of slavery, and he didn't seek to abolish the entrenched custom of male only leadership, correct?" Tommy asked.

"Yes."

"Did he mean for slavery to continue forever?"

"Objection, question is irrelevant and immaterial to the issues in this lawsuit," Renzulli said.

After a moment, Judge Bateman said, "The objection is sustained. Try to stay on track, Mr. O'Reilly."

"Yes, Your Honor. Now, Bishop Sierra, I believe you testified that the original apostles became ordained as priests at the last Supper. Is that correct?"

"Yes."

"Would women have also been present at the Last Supper?"

"I don't know," Bishop Sierra responded.

Tommy looked at Bishop Sierra with a puzzled look on his face and said, "I believe you said that Jesus treated women equally with men and that they were included as part of his disciples. Is that true?"

"Yes, I said that."

"Would the apostles have cooked the meal, or would women have prepared it in the time of Jesus?" Tommy asked.

"The women, most certainly," Sierra answered.

"Would Jesus have thrown the women out of the meal after they had prepared it, or would he have treated them equally with the men, as you have said was his custom?" Tommy asked.

"I don't know," Bishop Sierra responded.

"You seem to have a very convenient knowledge depending on the question, don't you, Bishop Sierra?" Tommy said with exasperation.

Monsignor Renzulli jumped to his feet and cried, "Objection!"

"Sustained! The jury will ignore that last comment by Mr. O'Reilly," Judge Bateman said.

Turning to Tommy O'Reilly with a strong glare, Judge Bateman said sternly, "Mr. O'Reilly, I'm warning you, any more gratuitous comments like the last one will be dealt with harshly. Do we understand each other?"

"Yes, Your Honor," Tommy said meekly.

Then turning to Bishop Sierra, he said, "Bishop Sierra, assuming Jesus followed his usual customs and women were present at the meal, could not he had been speaking to them as well when he said, 'Do this in remembrance of me'?"

"No."

"It is not possible?" Tommy asked

Bishop Sierra said sternly, "No, it's not possible!"

When Tommy began referring to his notes, Judge Bateman glanced at the clock and asked O'Reilly, "Mr. O'Reilly, are you at a point where this would be a good time for a recess?"

"Yes, Your Honor. It is."

"In that event, this court is recessed for thirty minutes until three thirty," Judge Bateman said.

CHAPTER THIRTY-FIVE

After the recess the court was back in session, and Tommy O'Reilly continued his cross-examination of Bishop Sierra.

"Bishop Sierra, I would like to take you to the Catholic feast of Pentecost. What do the Scriptures and the Catholic Church say happened on that day?"

Bishop Sierra answered, "Jesus had arisen from the dead, and all the disciples were gathered in a locked upper room because they were afraid of reprisals from the Jews. Jesus walked through the walls and the locked doors and breathed the Holy Spirit upon them."

After several moments of silence, Tommy asked, "Is that all that happened at that time? Is that it?"

"I don't know what you mean by your question," Bishop Sierra responded.

"Did not Jesus also say, 'Whose sins you shall forgive, they are forgiven, and whose sins you shall retain, they are retained,' to all those in the room?"

"Yes, he did."

"Are those words the foundation for the Sacrament of Penance for the Catholic Church?"

R.A. BROWN

"Yes, it is one of the foundations," Sierra answered.

"Are priests the only ones who can administer the Sacrament of Penance or Reconciliation?"

"Yes."

"And the power to administer the Sacrament of Penance in which the penitent is forgiven his or her sins was given to those to those in the room that day and has since been passed on to their successors, correct?" Tommy asked.

Bishop Sierra stirred in his chair, looked at Monsignor Renzulli, who stared right back at him, and then said, "Yes."

"At the time of the Pentecost, were the disciples following the example of Jesus and treating women equally, or had they reverted to their old ways of excluding them? In other words, were women present when Christ conferred the powers of the Sacrament of Penance?" Tommy asked.

Bishop Sierra knew Tommy had boxed him in. If women were present, they could arguably have received priestly orders for the Sacrament of Penance as well as the men. If women were not there, the apostles had reverted to their social customs of excluding women, which could account for the early church not appointing women to be priests.

"The Scriptures do not say specifically one way or the other," Bishop Sierra said.

"So, women might have been there, correct?"

"Yes."

"When Jesus conferred the priestly orders of the Sacrament of Penance on all the people in the room, if women had been there they would have received those orders as well, correct?"

"No."

"Why not? Did he say, 'All you *men* whose sins you shall forgive,' or did he say 'all *you* whose sins you shall forgive'?"

"Mr. O'Reilly, you're taking scripture out of context," Bishop Sierra said heatedly. "As I have said, when the Scriptures are taken as a whole, it is clear that the intent of Jesus was to restrict the priesthood to that of men only. You cannot just single out phrases and look at them without taking the Scriptures as a whole!"

"Yes, Bishop Sierra, that's indeed what you have said," Tommy said, looking at the jury with a bemused look. "Now please answer my question, and tell us what the Catholic Scriptures say Jesus said. 'All you *men* whose sins you shall forgive' or 'all *you* whose sins you shall forgive'?"

"The second one," Sierra responded.

"Now let's go to another dogma of the church. Would you explain to the jury what church dogma is?" Tommy said.

"Yes. I will be happy to." Looking at the jury, Sierra said, "Church dogma is a fundamental belief of the church. Dogma is an infallible teaching that cannot be ignored, which includes the required gender of priests."

"Is it a dogma of the Catholic Church that men and women are equal in the eyes of God?"

"Yes, it is."

"Bishop Sierra, on the one hand, you have a fundamental belief that men and women are equal in the eyes of God, but to be a representative of Jesus on earth, women are not equal to men to have the honor to serve as the representative of Jesus. Do you not see a conflict between these infallible truths of the church?"

"No, I do not," Bishop Sierra said firmly.

Tommy responded heatedly, "I submit there is an obvious conflict between the two dogmas, and that one of them just has to be wrong! One is based upon the teaching and example of Jesus, and the other is based upon not what he said, but what he didn't say. Don't you agree there's a conflict?"

"No, I do not!"

Tommy looked at the jury and rolled his eyes and looked back to Bishop Sierra and said, "One last question, Bishop Sierra. You've been here during the entire trial, have you not?"

"Yes, you know I have."

"Do you remember when Monsignor Renzulli objected to the question I asked Ms. Kowalski about whether she knew if God wanted her to be a priest?"

"Yes."

"Do you remember that Monsignor Renzulli said that Ms. Kowalski could not possibly know what was in the mind of God and that was outside her scope of knowledge?" Tommy asked.

"Yes," Bishop Sierra answered.

"Now I ask you, how can you and the other men of the Catholic Church possibly know what's in the mind of God concerning the gender of his priests?"

Bishop Sierra took a moment and said, "The Catholic Church is the embodiment of the Word and will of God on earth. When Jesus made Peter his first pope, the Scriptures are clear that Peter had his power on earth and all of the popes, including the present one, are in direct succession to Peter. When the popes speak on matters of faith and morals, they are infallible in that pronouncement. They cannot do otherwise. They are guided by God in the form of the Holy Spirit, and what they say is the will of God. Not you, not me, nor anyone else but the pope! The pope has declared that the priesthood should be limited to the male gender based upon the clear example of Jesus, and that, Mr. O'Reilly, is the will of God!"

"Thank you, Bishop Sierra. I have no further questions."

"Do you have any questions on redirect, Monsignor Renzulli?" Judge Bateman asked.

"Yes, I do, Your Honor."

"Then you may proceed."

"Bishop Sierra," Monsignor O'Reilly began, "Mr. O'Reilly asked you about the equality of women within the church. Does the church consider women inferior to men?" Monsignor Renzulli asked.

"No, the church does not believe women are inferior. Women are not denied the priesthood because it was and is a plan of *men*, but because it was and is the plan of *God*. Women can do things that men cannot do such as give life. Men can never do that. The church has been overtly clear in many areas and in many things about the absolute equality of men and women. It's simply an historical fact and an unbroken tradition that women cannot be priests any more than men can bear human life. Jesus likens himself as the bridegroom and the church as the bride. Men have the means and protective aspects of a bridegroom, and a woman doesn't have those any more than a man has the instincts of a woman in giving birth and nurturing life," Bishop Sierra responded.

"Mr. O'Reilly has tried to make a point that the social customs of the day would have prevented Jesus Christ from appointing a woman to be an apostle. Do you agree with that statement?"

"No, I do not."

"Why do you not agree?"

"If one is a Christian, then one has to believe that Jesus Christ was God incarnate into man. If one is not a Christian, then what he did or did not do is of no relevance. As God, he could have chosen anyone he wanted to be an apostle, regardless of social restrictions, and his truth would have prevailed. His Word was truth. The fact he only named men as his apostles is part of his Word and is what the church has believed and taught for over two thousand years. All the other characteristics I was asked about were merely incidental and irrelevant. A woman cannot and will never be a priest," Bishop Sierra answered.

"The plaintiff has said if she had a sex operation, she would have the genitalia to be a priest. Is genitalia relevant to the priesthood?"

"No, it is not."

"Will you please explain your answer?"

"Gladly. The presence of male genitalia is only one of many characteristics of a man. Men and women have a totally different biology as a result of gender. Gender is fundamental to a human being. As an example, the brains of the two genders are different both chemically and structurally leading to different programming. Men are more aggressive, women more nurturing. Men are more individualistic, women more social. Men tend to rely more on thought, whereas women rely more on feelings. All one has to do is watch children at play. No one has to tell the girl to play with dolls or the boy to play with toy soldiers or trucks. A woman, no matter how many surgeries she has, is still a woman, and a man, no matter how many surgeries he has, is still a man. As I have said many times before, it is the will of Jesus, as shown by all of his actions from the Scriptures, that the priests in his church are to be of his gender, *a male.*"

Monsignor Renzulli looked at the jury for a moment, and being satisfied with what he saw, said, "No further questions, Your Honor."

"Do you have any further cross examination, Mr. O'Reilly?" Judge Bateman asked.

"Yes, Your Honor, I do," Tommy said. "Bishop Sierra, you have testified that the basic qualifications for an applicant to the seminary and the priesthood are an unmarried male baptized in the Catholic Church. Is that correct?"

"Yes."

"It has come to my attention that you have ordained married males. Is that correct?" Tommy asked cryptically.

Bishop Sierra looked puzzled, and then he appeared to recognize where Tommy was going but needed time to formulate an answer. "I'm not sure what you mean. Perhaps you can jog my memory."

"I will be glad to, Bishop Sierra. Have you not ordained a married Episcopal priest into the priesthood of the Catholic Church?"

"Yes."

"Would you explain to the jury how this is possible given the basic qualifications you just told the jury?"

"The Episcopalian religion is quite similar in all respects to the Catholic religion except for their allegiance to the pope. The pope has given special dispensation to ordain married Episcopal priests when circumstances warrant including a vow of papal allegiance," Bishop Sierra answered.

"The Episcopalian religion also ordains women priests, does it not?"

"I believe it does."

"Will the Catholic Church ordain a female priest of the Episcopal religion, married or unmarried?"

"No."

"So is it your testimony that you and the Pope and the other cardinals have found a way to bend the rules to allow married male Episcopal priests to be ordained despite the basic qualifications! Yet you will not afford the same accommodation to a woman in the same circumstances just because she is a woman and not a man?" Tommy asked incredulously.

There was a long moment of silence, and Tommy said, "Never mind, Bishop Sierra, I withdraw the question. We already know your answer." Tommy looked at the jury in a disgusted way.

Turning again to Bishop Sierra, he said, "I have one more question, Bishop Sierra. Does the Catholic Church believe it is the church established by Jesus Christ?"

"Yes, it does."

"Is it fair to say that the Catholic Church considers itself to be the one, true Christian church?"

"It is the only church that has not wavered from the example and teachings of Jesus Christ from then and until now," Bishop Sierra said calmly.

"No further questions, Your Honor," Tommy said.

"Monsignor Renzulli, do you have any further questions for Bishop Sierra?" Judge Bateman asked.

"No, Your Honor."

Judge Bateman continued, "We are close to five o'clock. This court will adjourn until tomorrow morning at nine o'clock, when we will have closing arguments of counsel, and the jury will retire to deliberate in conformance with the instructions I will give to the jury."

"All rise," the bailiff said, and Judge Bateman left the bench and retired to his chambers.

Michael rose with the others when requested and left the courtroom. He made his way through the TV reporters who were reporting on the happenings in the courtroom on that day, and Michael was infuriated. The heretic lawyer for the heretic woman had made Bishop Sierra look like a fool. *How could such an imbecile become archbishop and a cardinal of his church?* he thought. Michael could have answered O'Reilly's questions a hundred times better on cross-examination than the bishop, and Monsignor Renzulli's strategy to rely on Bishop Sierra to prove his case had obviously backfired.

God was calling Michael to act, and he was ready! The Taser he had purchased had been powering all day. He prayed it would work and knew God would make sure it did. In his position, Michael had found out that the heretic lived in a nunnery with two Sisters of Mercy whose mission was at Mercy Hospital. Tonight was the night when he and God would make their move, and again he felt his excitement building.

CHAPTER THIRTY-SIX

Tommy was working on the points that he wanted to make in his closing argument the next day when his telephone rang at ten thirty p.m.

"Hello, this is Tommy O'Reilly," he said.

"Mr. O'Reilly, this is Sister Agnes. I'm a nun who lives with Aleksandra Kowalski," the other voice said.

"Yes, Sister Agnes, I know who you are. What can I do for you?"

"Is Alex with you, Mr. O'Reilly?" she said with alarm.

"No. Should she be?" Tommy answered.

"I don't know," she said louder.

"What's happened, Sister Agnes?"

"Alex received a call from a lawyer in your office, Gerald Grant. He said he was outside our house and had an important document from you to give to her. She was to read it and call you immediately afterward."

"What! Sister Agnes, where is Alex?"

"We don't know. That's why we called you, Mr. O'Reilly. After about ten minutes, she didn't come inside, and we went outside to look for her. When we couldn't find her, that's when I called you," she said.

"Sister Agnes, are you going to be there for a while?"

"Yes, Sister Caroline and I have day shifts this month," she replied.

"Don't move. The police will be in touch with you shortly!" Tommy said.

"The police!" she said. "Do you think something bad has happened to Alex?"

"Something has happened, Sister Agnes. And I can't imagine anything about it being good. Don't move, and stay by the phone!" Tommy said, and then he hung up.

Roy Yardley answered his house phone on the third ring. "This had better be good, Tommy" reading his caller ID. "I'm about to go to bed."

"Roy, my client, Aleksandra Kowalski, is missing, and I think she may have been kidnapped."

Roy immediately became serious. "Tell me what you know, Tommy."

Tommy related his conversation with Sister Agnes. "Do you have contact information for her family and close friends in the event she wanted to go somewhere and chill out for a while?" Yardley asked.

"I have all of her files here. I'm at home working on closing arguments for tomorrow." Tommy relayed Yardley the information he had requested. "Roy, I know her very well, and she's not hiding somewhere to chill out. Something has happened to her, and whatever it is, it's not a good thing."

"I have to run all of the normal traps first, Tommy, before I can go to an emergency setting. I will do the best I can in the fastest time I can and will call you back when I either know something or when we go to plan B. Good enough?"

"Yes, Roy, that's good enough. And, Roy…"

"Yeah, Tommy?"

"Thanks."

"Don't mention it. Now get off the phone so I can get to work."

The nights Tommy was in trial he could seldom sleep well because of the adrenaline flow. This was worse than any of those nights. He tried some Black Bush and a cigar to settle his nerves, but it didn't work. At five thirty a.m. his phone rang.

"Tommy, this is Roy. We've contacted everyone we can, and we can't find any trace of her. She's simply vanished. I have a priority e-mail in to Chief DiFrates to meet with him in a couple of hours. I've requested his consideration to initiate the Gulf Coast Task Force. It has been designed for situations like this, high profile with a high degree of urgency. If he agrees to do this, the task force will consist of all of the police agencies located in the Gulf Coast area, including the Houston Police Department, the Harris County Sheriff's Department, the Highway Patrol, the Texas Rangers, and the FBI. It has been designed to have one central command into which all agents and officers report so as to avoid bureaucratic channels."

"When will you know if he will initiate the task force?" Tommy asked.

"The meeting should take no more than an hour. When are you due in court?" Yardley inquired.

"At nine a.m.," Tommy responded.

"I'll call you before you get into court." And with that he hung up.

When Manuel dropped Tommy at the rear entrance of the federal building that morning at eight thirty, his cell phone rang.

"Tommy, this is Roy. The chief has initiated the Gulf Coast Task Force. It will be run by the Houston Police Department, and the man in charge of it is Sergeant Sam Pierce, a thirty-year veteran of the force. I know Sam well and there's not a better person to lead this effort. We're operating under the assumption she's still in the area, but we also have the FBI in case someone took her out of state. The local FBI office will be coordinating with other FBI offices. We'll find her, Tommy," and he hung up. As Tommy went into the federal building, he knew they would eventually find her—but in what shape, and when?

CHAPTER THIRTY-SEVEN

Alex was asleep; or knocked out. She did not know which and didn't care. She only knew she was out of it and was trying not to be. She began to clear the cobwebs, and her mind started to swim to reach the surface of awareness. She didn't know where she was, but she felt her face resting on something. She moved her head and knew it was not a pillow. Whatever it was, it was rough to her skin. She tried to move her arms and legs, but they felt pinned down. She looked down and saw that her head had been lying on a piece of unfinished lumber; under it her arms and legs were in wooden stocks! She tried to pull her arms and legs free, but the openings were not big enough. Her legs were lying on a wide bench attached at right angles to the leg stocks, and it was wide enough for her to sit on. When she leaned backward, she noticed there was nothing behind her back to support it.

What a diabolical trap! she thought. Whoever did this made sure she would remain in an upright sitting position indefinitely. She was in good physical shape, but she realized her lower back was starting to ache.

She began to take note of her surroundings. It was dark around her with only a strange flickering glow. Stars? No, she knew she was not outside. The lights were in the distance in front of her, not above. The lights were from candles, a lot of candles. She began to feel fear. Not the fear of something that she could recognize, like a spider or a snake. She was afraid of those things, but those fears could be rationalized. This was a different fear, something unknown. Something that she knew could cause her greater harm. She knew instinctively that whoever was responsible for this did not like her at all. Whatever plans they had for her were worse than any of her fears that could be rationalized. Fear transformed into terror.

She shuddered involuntarily. "Get a grip," she told herself. *Whatever threat that is here has to be from a human, and humans can be dealt with,* she thought with some conviction. Surely whatever was happening had to be some kind of mistake or joke. Who was she kidding? This was too cruel to be a joke, so it had to be a horrible mistake.

"*Agnus dei…agnus dei…agnus dei.*" The sound of her heart pounding in her chest was being replaced by an eerie chanting sound. "*Agnus dei… agnus dei… agnus dei.*"

As the chant continued, she recognized the words as Latin meaning, "The Lamb of God." As she peered intently into the darkness for a clue, a dark rectangular shape came into focus. The flickering glow of light around it seemed to reflect off a shiny surface. It appeared to be situated on a slightly raised platform of some kind. Her mind began to search for answers. An altar with candles. There was just enough light that she could barely see a reflection in the shiny surface. She squinted, trying to identify what seemed to be a large black cross reflecting off the floor. Hope began to surge. An altar and a cross. She had to be in a Christian church. Thank God! What harm could possibly come to her in a church?

As the drone of the chant became louder, the cross reflected on the floor began to move. Her mind must be playing tricks on her. Or maybe it wasn't a cross at all. It was a silhouette, a dark silhouette of a person in black garb lying prostrate on the floor with outspread arms. As the eerie chant pounded louder in her ears, the cross disappeared, and a large man rose up in front of her. He was dressed in a priest's cassock or a monk's robes, she could not tell which. He had a full black beard, a completely shaved head, and candlelight sparkled in a pair of intense, coal black eyes. Priest's robes or not, in the dark room in front of the black polished altar, the figure appeared satanic in the dim glow of the candles. Terror began to tear away at the hope she had left.

"Who are you?" she rasped in a voice she barely recognized.

"I am the instrument of the Lamb of God," a low voice growled.

As her mind raced to approach this rationally, she summoned all her internal reserves, which she was surprised to find intact.

"And just what does that have to do with me?" she said in a bold voice, trying to sound as normal as possible.

"What does that have to do with you?" he screamed. "Heretic! You're a heretic! There's only one answer for heresy! Repentance and absolution for your sins! A heretic must achieve total remorse! Total remorse can be obtained only through the penance of pain!" he yelled, spittle flying from his mouth.

As he closed his eyes and took a deep breath, he enunciated his words in a more somber tone, "I will be the instrument for your penance through pain. I will work with you until you have renounced your sins and have begged God for forgiveness and mercy. Once he has told me your soul has been cleansed, you will exit this life free of sin, to be reunited with the Lamb of God."

Her mind whirled as she tried to make some sense of all this. There had to be something she could do. This really could not be happening to her. She tried to be rational, but this was not rational.

"You're crazy!" she yelled back. "You have no right to do this!"

He shook his big head and looked pleadingly at her. "Yes, I have the right to do this. I am merely his instrument. Soon you will recognize this. His will be done."

And with that, he uncoiled his right hand from behind his back. Gripped tightly in his fist was a thick leather handle that sprouted frayed leather strands about a yard long. There were little metal balls on the ends of the leather strands that sparkled menacingly in the diffused candlelight. As he stepped close to her, fear rose like bile in her throat. She heard the leather crackle as he it whipped down her back. The little metal balls ripped through her blouse as if it were

176   R.A. BROWN

tissue paper and tore into her skin. The leather straps seared along her back once more, the metal balls again following dutifully to create rivulets of intense pain.

Her body began to convulse, and she screamed a scream no mortal should ever have to make. She felt hot tears flow down her cheek, and even hotter liquid began to flow down her back. Another crackle … more pain. As her tormentor wanted her to do, she began to pray. Not for the redemption he wanted, because she had nothing to repent. Instead she fervently whispered, *Please, God, please make this go away.* God answered her prayers. Her head fell limply to her chest, and she quickly collapsed into a total state of unfeeling oblivion.

CHAPTER THIRTY-EIGHT

When Tommy entered the courtroom, Monsignor Renzulli was seated along with his local counsel, but his adjunct was missing.

"Good morning, Monsignor Renzulli. Where is your shadow, Father Michael Murray?" Tommy asked.

Renzulli frowned at the reference but said, "He became quite ill last evening. He thinks it's food poisoning, so he won't be here today. Why are you interested?"

Tommy decided to press forward on more important issues and address the disappearance of Alex head on. "Never mind, I have something much more important to discuss. Monsignor Renzulli, I have some bad news that we need to bring to the attention of Judge Bateman. My client, Aleksandra Kowalski, is missing, and we think it's possibly a kidnapping!"

Startled, Monsignor Renzulli asked, "How do you know?"

Tommy related the events of the previous evening and the conversation he had just had with Roy Yardley.

Renzulli glared at O'Reilly and said, "O'Reilly, did she get cold feet, and are you hiding her somewhere? Is this something you've cooked up to try to lay blame on my clients? Is this something you are using to try and get the sympathy of the jury? If it is, this is pretty low, O'Reilly."

Tommy O'Reilly bristled, stood still, and stared for a very long minute at Monsignor Renzulli, and Renzulli held Tommy's stare. "I don't know what you think of me, Monsignor, but I know it isn't much," Tommy said angrily. "What I'm telling you is the absolute truth. Do you think I would go so far as to fraudulently initiate a Gulf Coast Task Force just to gain an advantage in a lawsuit? That would not only permanently cost me my license to practice law but garner me some time in the Huntsville state prison. That would be idiotic, and Monsignor, again, I don't know what you think of me, but I'm not an idiot!"

After a long, protracted stare, Monsignor Renzulli spoke. "Okay, O'Reilly, maybe I believe you. Now let's go see Judge Bateman and see if he believes you as well."

After arranging with the clerk to see Judge Bateman in chambers, they were escorted into the judge's inner sanctum and stood before Judge Bateman, who was seated at his desk in a suit and not in his judicial robes. Tommy thought how ordinary he looked dressed like this without his judicial attire. Judge Bateman looked up from his desk with a pen in hand and said, "Gentlemen, please sit down. What may I do for you? Have you come to advise me of a settlement?"

Tommy and Monsignor Renzulli set down in warm leather chairs placed before Judge Bateman's desk, and Tommy began. "Nothing quite as simple as that, Your Honor," and he again related the events of the previous evening and the call from Roy Yardley that he had received that morning.

Judge Bateman looked at them both for a while. He folded his hands in front of him, looked at them, and as he lifted his head, he said, "To say the least, this is highly unusual. I'll ask you first, Mr. O'Reilly, since you're counsel for the plaintiff. What do you want the court to do?"

Tommy thought a moment and answered, "Under the circumstances, judge, I would like a continuance until the plaintiff has been found. A party is entitled to be in court for all proceedings, and this is no different than if she had taken ill."

"I disagree with you, Mr. O'Reilly. A party is entitled to be in court for all testimony so they can assist counsel with direct and cross-examination of other witnesses. I'm not aware of any rule that requires a party to be present for closing arguments and/or for the rendering of verdict. After the conclusion of testimony, they become bystanders like anyone else, albeit obviously more interested than anyone else."

"I would like time to research that point and file a brief, Your Honor," Tommy said.

Judge Bateman growled, "We don't have the time, counselor. I have to keep my docket moving. Request denied. Monsignor Renzulli, what are your thoughts?"

"Your Honor, any stay in the proceedings because of unknown reasons for the plaintiff's disappearance will undoubtedly be prejudicial to my clients. Doubtless there will be those who will think my clients had something to do with her disappearance to prevent her from continuing her pursuit to become a seminarian and ultimately a priest. While nothing could be farther from the truth, the inference could be made, and that could be highly prejudicial."

Judge Bateman thought a moment and then said, "Yes, Monsignor, I see your point, and it's a good one. Mr. O'Reilly, what is your response?"

Tommy decided to ad lib, "It's quite common for the task force to find someone within twenty-four hours." Tommy hoped that was true. "If not, then it might be days or weeks. Let's see what we can find out tomorrow and then go from there."

Judge Bateman looked at both of them and said, "I believe both of you gentlemen are overlooking the obvious."

Tommy looked at Monsignor Renzulli, who looked back at Tommy, and then they both turned to look at Judge Bateman with confused looks on their faces.

"Don't get me wrong," Judge Bateman said, alternatively looking at Tommy then Monsignor Renzulli. "I'm not trying to be overly dramatic, but practical. If indeed Ms. Kowalski was abducted, the person or persons who abducted her obviously do not have her best interest at heart. If the police find her in the next twenty-four hours, she is just as likely to be dead as alive. That's the only way they can absolutely ensure that she does not attain her goal of becoming a priest. Do you agree with what I'm saying?"

Tommy felt an inward shudder, but both he and Monsignor Renzulli continued to look at Judge Bateman.

Judge Bateman continued, "By your silence, I assume you both agree that what I have described is a real possibility. If she is found dead within the next twenty-four hours, we will not need to continue with jury argument and jury deliberation. Although it would be a horrible and tragic outcome, as a practical matter, she would have no legal right to pursue her quest to attend the seminary. If she's found alive within the next twenty-four hours, then we can proceed as planned. If her situation is unknown at this time tomorrow, we could still proceed to the jury without her. I believe that's the best solution for all concerned, to stay the proceedings for the next twenty-four hours."

Both lawyers considered Bateman's comments for a moment, then Renzulli asked, "What about possible prejudice to my clients, Your Honor?"

"I will instruct the jury that they are not to assume that your clients had anything to do with her disappearance or that Mr. O'Reilly has anything to do with it either to gain their sympathy." Judge Bateman had obviously thought what Monsignor Renzulli had originally thought.

Bateman continued, "I will instruct them that they are to consider the evidence without regard to the plaintiff's absence being caused by the influence of you, your clients, or Mr. O'Reilly. If the jury finds for the defendants, then the trial will be over. If the jury finds for the plaintiff, then I can postpone my decision on the mandatory injunction until she reappears. If she's ultimately found dead, then I won't have to rule on the mandatory injunction, because I couldn't very well order the defendants to accept a dead person to their seminary. If she's found alive, then the circumstances of her disappearance will then be known."

Looking straight at Tommy O'Reilly, the judge said, "Depending upon the circumstances of her disappearance, I would be then able to rule on injunctive relief." The implications were clear: if Tommy had hidden her out and he had a jury verdict in her favor, Judge Bateman wasn't going to rule until she was found, and the reason for her disappearance had better have been outside of Tommy's or Alex's control.

"As a result, these proceedings are adjourned until nine tomorrow morning. Let us all hope that the task force is successful in determining the whereabouts of Miss Kowalski. If there are no other questions, I will see you gentlemen in the morning," Judge Bateman said.

Tommy and Monsignor Renzulli left the chambers of Judge Bateman and went back into the courtroom. Tommy went to the plaintiffs table, grabbed his things, and said, "Come on, Silk! We've got twenty-four hours to find Alex!"

CHAPTER THIRTY-NINE

When Manuel dropped Tommy and Willis off at the office, the satellite trucks and reporters were back in full force. The news of Alex's disappearance had obviously gotten out to the media. He assumed, and rightly so, the task force had put her picture out to the TV stations with a request for people to be on the watch for her. The off-duty policemen at Tommy's had their hands full this morning controlling the crowd. Questions were shouted at Tommy from the street in such a cacophony that he was unable to recognize anyone individually. Then he had an idea. He stopped and abruptly turned around.

"Quiet, please," he said. "I have a statement to make."

There was immediate silence.

"Ms. Kowalski has been abducted, and we can only assume that whoever has her means her great harm. The Gulf Coast Task Force has been initiated to find her. If anyone, I mean anyone, has any thoughts on where she might be or who may have done this horrible act, please call the Houston Police Department and ask for Lieutenant Sam Pierce. He's coordinating the search for her.

"I want everyone to know this is not something I'm involved in as a trial ploy to gain sympathy from the jury. I also want everyone to know that I believe the Catholic Church is not involved in this in any way. This is a real, and I repeat, real, emergency. This is the act of a sick individual or individuals, and surely someone out there knows somebody whose twisted beliefs would cause them to do this.

"Please think about what I've said and think about it diligently. If you're aware of anybody who's likely to do something like this, please call the Houston Police Department. Please help us. Thank you. That's all I have."

Tommy immediately turned and walked into the office, followed by Willis. The ever-present Betty was there, and "Hello, boss," was all she said.

"Do you have any news?" he asked.

"No, I don't," she said, and then paused a second before continuing. "Don't worry, boss. They'll find her."

"Thanks, Betty." And he and Willis went into his office.

"Tommy, what you said out there gave me an idea," Willis began after they were seated. "You're a Catholic, and I agree that the Catholic Church would not be involved in this. But as a Catholic, are you aware of any right-wing factions of the Catholic Church in the Houston area? This obviously has to be the work of somebody who is a Catholic but an extremist who believes they have to prevent Alex from entering the seminary. It has to be a psychotic Catholic, and I believe we need to start with extreme schisms if they exist."

Tommy thought a moment and then said, "I don't know of any groups like that, Silk, but you make a good point." He picked up his intercom and asked Betty to call Monsignor Renzulli at the headquarters of the archdiocese.

A few minutes later Betty rang on the intercom. "Monsignor Renzulli is holding for you, boss."

Tommy picked up the phone and said, "Hello, Monsignor Renzulli," and without waiting for a reply continued, "I'll get right to the point. Is the archdiocese aware of any right-wing fringe groups of the Catholic Church in the Houston area?"

There was a long silence before Monsignor Renzulli answered. "I appreciate what you said, Mr. O'Reilly, to the media about the church and it not being involved in this horrible abduction. As you know, I'm from Washington and not from here. Let me ask around, and I'll call you back."

"What did he say, Tommy?"

"He said he would ask around to see if anybody knows of extremist groups out there and will call me back."

"What should we do in the meantime?"

Tommy sighed. "Just wait."

Thirty minutes later, Betty called on the intercom and said, "Monsignor Renzulli is on the line again for you, boss."

Tommy grabbed his phone. "What have you found out, Monsignor?" Tommy asked urgently.

"There's a church in downtown Houston named the Church of the Holy Rosary. The pastor is a Jesuit by the name of Father Holmes. They've avoided the changes instituted by Vatican II. In other words, they still say mass in Latin, require women to have their heads covered and wear veils at Mass, allow only the priests to distribute communion, and pretty much everything that the church did before the reforms they still do. If there's a group like you asked about, Father Holmes might know where you could look."

"Thanks, Monsignor," Tommy replied. "However, I doubt if he would take my call. Because of the lawsuit, I don't have the best reputation among Catholic priests. Would you please consider setting up an appointment for me?"

After a moment Renzulli said, "Yes, I will do that, O'Reilly. When do you want it?"

"As soon as possible!" Tommy said.

"I will put you on hold and make the call," Monsignor Renzulli replied. After an interminably long few minutes, Renzulli came back on the phone. "Father Holmes will see you as soon as you can get there."

"Thank you, Monsignor Renzulli," Tommy said sincerely.

"You're welcome, Mr. O'Reilly. And…" Monsignor Renzulli hesitated.

"Yes?" Tommy asked.

"Good luck."

R.A. BROWN

CHAPTER FORTY

The Church of the Holy Rosary was in an older part of downtown Houston. Tommy and Willis went to the rectory and announced themselves. The young priest who was the assistant to Father Holmes was none too happy to see them, but he nevertheless showed the men to Father Holmes's office.

The assistant opened the door and led them in. Father Holmes was sitting behind his desk with his hands folded in front of him with only what could be politely called a scowl on his face. People awaiting a root canal would look happier. He didn't ask them to sit down, and standing before his desk reminded Tommy of being called to the principal's office. Father Holmes went right to the point.

"I don't like you, O'Reilly, not in the least bit. You're a Catholic pursuing one of the greatest offenses against Holy Mother Church that I have ever witnessed! I detest what you're trying to do, and I wouldn't have granted you an appointment or even so much as looked at you but for the intervention of Monsignor Renzulli. What do you have in mind? And make it snappy! You have five minutes," Father Holmes concluded and began looking at his watch.

"Father, I understand your feelings. Believe me, I do. I would probably feel the same way if I was sitting on your side of the desk. But I'm not. I'm on this side, and I'm asking you to set your feelings aside for a minute. A young woman is missing and is most likely in mortal danger. Regardless of what you think of her or me, she deserves a chance to live, and you might be able to help," Tommy pleaded.

Father Holmes looked up, and asked, "Me? How can I help?"

At least he's not timing me now, Tommy thought. "Father, whoever abducted Ms. Kowalski did it for one purpose only: to stop her from becoming a priest and not in any lawful way. I know the Catholic Church would not be involved in something like this nor would it sanction these horrible actions. But whoever did this is probably Catholic, because only a Catholic would have an interest in stopping her." Now came the tricky part.

"That leads to the question of what kind of Catholic would go to such extreme means. We think it's possible that it's the work of some right-wing extreme fringe group unsanctioned by the Catholic Church, if indeed such a group exists. The people in such a group would undoubtedly consider themselves to be very devout and would attend Mass regularly."

Tommy took a deep breath and said quietly, "Since these people would be extremely conservative in their approach to Catholicism, we think it's possible that they would come to Holy Rosary for the sacraments, since your parish has not adopted the reforms of Vatican II."

Father Holmes grew red in the face, and a vein began pulsing in his neck. "How dare you even suggest that one of my parishioners could be involved in something as terrible as this?" he bellowed. "The fact we pursue a liturgy that is the way the Catholic Church worshiped for thousands of years instead of the last sixty years doesn't make us terrorists!"

"Father Holmes, I'm not suggesting that you or your parish isn't fervent or devout in its beliefs," Tommy said calmly. "This may be the act of one or two individuals whose beliefs are so twisted that they would think they are doing God's work to abduct Miss Kowalski. I only think it's reasonable that they would prefer a liturgy of the old school such as yours. Please give it some thought. That's all I ask. A young woman's life is at stake, and I don't believe someone as devout and sincere as you would want her death on their conscience."

Father Holmes looked hard at Tommy for what to Tommy seemed minutes but in actuality was only seconds. Finally he said with less anger, "Okay, I'll think about it. That's all I will commit to." Then looking at his watch he said, "Is that all? I'm very busy, if you must know."

"Yes, Father, that's all, and thanks for your time. We both greatly appreciate you giving what we said some thought." He stuck his hand out to shake that of Father Holmes, but it was ignored. They turned around, and the young priest who had been standing behind them led them out of the office and to the front door. When they got to the door, the young Jesuit handed them a card and said, "Call my cell in thirty minutes. I may have something, and I don't want to talk here." The card said William Reiner, S.J.

As Manuel drove Willis and Tommy back to the office, Willis asked Tommy, "What do you make of that?"

"The old Jesuit, Holmes, he wouldn't spit on us if we were on fire, and it's not that he wouldn't like spitting on us. The young Jesuit, I don't know. He's a priest like all the rest of them, but maybe we said something that hit home when we were talking to the old guy. Let's just hope he knows something and is willing to share it."

When they arrived at the office, Tommy and Willis went to Tommy's office and called Father Reiner's cell number on the speaker phone. After a few rings a man answered, "Hello?"

"Father Reiner?"

"Yes it is."

"This is Tommy O'Reilly, Father, and I have you on a speakerphone with Mr. Thompson, whom you met earlier. You said to call you."

"Yes I did," Reiner said and paused, clearly nervous. "I want you to know that I share the feelings of Father Holmes about your conduct, and I pray as often as I can that you won't be successful in your efforts. But having said that, I don't believe murder is the way to achieve God's will." Then there was silence.

"Father Reiner?" Willis asked. "Are you there?"

"Yes I am still here," the young priest said quietly. "I am by nature non-judgmental, and my Jesuit training has made me more so, so what I am about to say is difficult for me."

"We understand, Father. We will use whatever you tell us with the greatest of caution and diligence," Tommy said.

"Thank you. Well then … there is a group called Congratio Agnus Dei, which in English means 'Associates of the Lamb of God.' They are a very small group, maybe a dozen or so, and the group is led by Michael Vargas. Vargas was apparently left some family money sometime back, so he's comfortable enough that he doesn't seem to need to work. I understand that he applied to the seminary more than once but was not accepted. The rumors are that it was for psychological reasons. He has never gotten over the rejection and even wears the cassock of a priest but without the Roman collar whenever he attends Mass. Father Holmes lets him get away with it, but I think it is very weird. Even without the Roman collar, some people can mistake him for a priest, which is what I think Vargas is attempting to do. I think he fits the profile you described to Father Holmes.

"He attends Mass at the church every weekday and all, not just one, but *all* of the masses on Sunday in that cassock of his. He also writes a newspaper for Agnus Dei, which he sends out monthly, which advocates changes in the church that would take it back centuries. He has obtained a list of all the Catholics in the archdiocese somehow so he must have connections there and sends his newspaper out free of charge. I don't want to accuse anybody of anything, and I am not saying that group had anything to do with this. Do you understand?"

"Yes, Father, we do."

After your conversation with Father Holmes, it occurred to me that Vargas might know something … I believe I would start with Congratio Agnus Dei if I were you."

"Thank you very much, Father Holmes. Believe me, we will tread very carefully," Tommy said sincerely. "I appreciate this very much."

"Don't thank me, O'Reilly. I'm not doing this for you. I detest what you're doing and your motives for doing so. However, I'm a Christian, and what I'm doing is the Christian thing to do. I'm doing this for someone greater than you and greater than you could ever be," Father Reiner said quietly and then hung up.

"Silk, now let's see what we can find out about the Associates of the Lamb of God and one Michael Vargas!"

CHAPTER FORTY-ONE

Tommy and Willis went online and researched the Associates of the Lamb of God. This led them to a website for the organization that advocated a number of changes that the Catholic Church should adopt. Each change was accompanied by scriptural references and historical references that the Associates of the Lamb of God believed supported their argument for the change. There was also a picture of Michael Vargas. He was heavyset, bald, with deep-set brown eyes, and heavily bearded. He indeed was wearing a priest's cassock in the picture but without the Roman collar.

"I recognize this person, Tommy!" Willis said. "While you've been focused on the trial, I've had an opportunity to observe the spectators in the courtroom. This guy is part of the press corps, and he's been in the courtroom every minute during the trial. He probably got his press credentials because of his newspaper. He hasn't been wearing the cassock, only street clothes, but he has a face that I'm not likely to forget."

They noted the address of the headquarters of the Associates the Lamb of God and called the Houston Police Department and asked for Lieutenant Sam Pierce. After a few minutes, they were put through.

"Lieutenant Pierce, Mr. O'Reilly. How may I assist you?"

"I think I may have a lead on who might have something to do with Aleksandra Kowalski's disappearance," Tommy answered hurriedly. Then Tommy told him about his conversation with Father Reiner and what he and Silk had found on the Internet.

After a moment of contemplation, Lieutenant Pierce said, "That's very circumstantial, Mr. O'Reilly. We could send a cruiser by to talk with Mr. Vargas, but if he's involved, he probably wouldn't say anything. He might even lawyer up. And we'd need something a lot more tangible in order to get a search warrant."

"What do you need?" Tommy asked urgently. "My gut's telling me this guy knows something."

"You're a lawyer, Mr. O'Reilly. You know what we need, and it's more than a gut feeling. We need something specific. We need some hard evidence that ties in Vargas to Ms. Kowalski."

After a moment to absorb what Pierce said, Tommy said, "Hypothetically, Lieutenant, let's say I find something specific and tangible that does just that but perhaps is obtained in a way that would not be totally within a police officer's handbook. How soon can you get a search warrant?"

Pierce thought a moment and then said "We can do it real quick. You're not a police officer, and hypothetically speaking, if you come across some tangible evidence, we wouldn't ask you how it came into your possession. We're not required by law to do so. You'd only have to tell me what you have. The only requirement for a warrant is that the affiant, that being you, is reliable, and since you're a lawyer, who, by definition is an officer of the court, I would consider you reliable. If you were to call me and tell me what you have, I'd present it to one of the DAs, which we have here twenty-four hours, seven days a week. He or she would draft the warrant and present it to one of the two magistrates, who are also here twenty-four-seven. The warrant would be issued either as a right to search or a warrant to arrest. The whole process will take about ten minutes, tops.

"Once I have the warrant in my hands I can call task force officers to respond instead of going through different enforcement agencies' communication links in the different vehicles. All members of the task force carry Nextel. This speeds up what would otherwise be a bureaucratic process. All you have to do is swear that you have the tangible evidence. I'll verify you as a reliable source and enlist the tangible evidence in my request for a warrant. I hope I've made myself clear," Lieutenant Pierce concluded.

"Thank you, Lieutenant," Tommy responded gracefully. "I'll let you know if and when I find something."

"Mr. O'Reilly, please be careful," Pierce said cautiously. "I don't know what you are up to but whoever's behind this, promises to be a very bad person."

Tommy O'Reilly hung up and said, "Let's go, Silk. We'll take the Navigator instead of having Manuel drive us. It'll be less conspicuous than the town car."

"Where are we going?" Willis asked as they were hurrying out the door.

"We're going to the headquarters of the Associates of the Lamb of God. I'm convinced they know where Alex is, or they know someone who does!"

So much for the promise of treading carefully, Willis thought.

CHAPTER FORTY-TWO

The Heights was an old residential neighborhood five miles northwest of downtown Houston, and as they pulled up to the address Tommy said, "Silk, the Heights is a perfect place for the Lamb of God's head-quarters. The building we are looking at would draw attention a lot of places, but not here." The Heights had been a pre-World II residential area close to downtown, which had been attractive due to its higher elevation as a protection against the ubiquitous Houston flooding, and hence its name. With the recent resurgence in inner city living, new construction had sprung up next to old construction. With the afflu-ent living among the less fortunate, the Heights was a melting pot of housing design. The building that headquartered the Associates of the Lamb of God was a small single-story bungalow of gray adobe. It looked like some of the other old homes on the street except for a magnificent cross that stood atop the tiled roof over the porch, and even with the cross, it blended in.

"What're we going to do, Tommy?"

"We're going to ring the doorbell and see if Vargas answers. If he's the one who has Alex, then she must be with him. If he answers the door, we'll bluff our way in and then see if we can find any tangible evidence that she's here."

Willis said, "He's been at the trial, so he'll recognize us. How're we going to get in?"

"We'll make up something…We'll tell him Monsignor Renzulli is going to reference his newspaper tomorrow in closing argument and the law entitles us to talk to him. I don't know, Silk. After all, we're two against one."

"What if he isn't here?" Willis asked.

"We will go to plan B," Tommy said cryptically.

"What's that?"

"Silk, quit sounding like a lawyer," Tommy said angrily. "Come on. Let's go!"

They went to the door and rang the bell, waited a few moments, and rang again. When it appeared there was no one at the residence he tried turning the door. It was locked.

"What do we do now, Tommy? It might be time to haul out your plan B," Willis said sarcastically.

Tommy looked all around and turned back to Willis. "We're too obvious out here in front of the house, Silk. Let's go around back and see if we can find a way in."

"Oh, yeah, and *that's* not obvious, Tommy. We're a black man and a white man in suits sneaking around to the back of the house. We sure don't look like meter readers, you know," Willis said pointedly.

Tommy replied over his shoulder as he headed to the backyard, "Maybe we look like repo guys. With some of the people in *this* neighborhood, repo guys are the last thing they want to mess with. Let's go!"

They went around back and tried the back door, but it was locked also. Peering through the windows, they noticed they were the old slider-type with six windowpanes per window. The upper window locked into the lower window with a half-moon latch.

"Maybe we can break a pane of glass and reach in and unlock the window, raise it, and climb in," Tommy said.

"Sorry to rain on your parade, Tommy, but the house probably has an alarm," Willis said grimly.

"How would you know that, Silk?"

"You live in a high-rise with all those other rich people, and it has all that security, so you don't know about these things." Willis grinned. "Since I'm an affluent young lawyer with a growing family, we moved to one of those affluent young lawyer neighborhoods with growing families. I had to get an alarm. I was there when the alarm guy came out. See those metal strips between the window and the window pane?"

"Yeah, I see them," Tommy answered.

"They conduct electric current, and if anyone breaks the current while the alarm is on, the alarm will sound both here, which will alert the neighbors, and at the alarm provider's central command, after which they will alert the cops. Are you ready for cops at this point?" Willis asked.

Tommy rolled his eyes and said, "I hope there's something behind this dissertation on alarms."

"Of course," Willis said indignantly. "The alarm guy told me the way to bypass the alarm is to put aluminum foil between the two contact points, and you'll trick the current into thinking it's still on."

"It doesn't sound exactly like a foolproof system to me," Tommy said.

"That's why he told me, so he could talk me into adding a glass breakage feature. When the glass breaks it triggers the alarm. If this house has the glass breakage feature and we break the glass to bypass with foil between the contact points, the alarm will go off."

"How do we know if he is as smart as you and has it?" Tommy asked.

"We don't."

Tommy looked around the back of the house to see if he could find anything that could lead to a way in. After a moment he went to the back door and bent down and studied the space between the door and the door jamb. "Okay, Silk, the back door will have the same current passing from the door jam to the door, right?"

"It should." Willis replied

"Look at the door, Silk," Tommy said.

Willis bent down and saw that the door was an old, solid wood, six-panel door with an old-style lock.

"Silk, if we were to put a piece of aluminum into that space between the jamb and the door lock, would that fool the current from the jamb into thinking it was still in contact with the door?"

"Yes," Willis replied, "according to the alarm guy."

"This old lock looks like the lock they always push open with a credit card in the movies. Would the magnetic strip on a credit card fool the electric current if I got it just right between the two contact points?" Tommy asked.

"I don't know, Tommy."

"Okay, we can't risk it then," Tommy mused. "What we need is a piece of aluminum to wrap around something that we could use to push into the space between the door and the jam, like a credit card. We could push the door open, hold our tool there, close the door, and pull our tool out once we're inside."

He looked to Willis for confirmation, and Willis thought a moment, nodded, and said, "That could work... but you're responsible for posting bail if it doesn't!" He paused for a moment then continued, "So what are we going to use for this break-in tool which, if it doesn't work, will lead to our incarceration as felons and consequently the loss of our licenses to practice law?"

"Why ask me? You're smarter than I am—come up with something!"

CHAPTER FORTY-THREE

When they had returned from the convenience store around the corner, they had a large plastic spatula and a box of aluminum foil. Tommy had wrapped the spatula with aluminum foil, and they pushed it between the jam in the door at the latch, and it fit easily. With a loud click the door opened, and they did as Tommy had said they would do and went in and closed the door. They were in the kitchen, with no dishes in sight or any sign of breakfast.

"This guy is very neat, or he wasn't here last night," Willis said.

"Let's hope he isn't neat. Let's hope he was here with Alex last night. Let's hope she's still here, and he's gone," Tommy said.

They walked into a small living area, which was also quite tidy. Tommy yelled as loudly as he could "Alex! Alex, can you hear me?"

The house was silent as a tomb.

He turned to Willis. "Check the bedrooms, Silk, and look everywhere for any sign of Alex. Check the closets and drawers for anything that might be helpful. I'll check in desk over there."

Tommy went to the desk, and on top was something that gave him a chill, but at the same time gave him hope that they were on the right track. On top of the desk were articles out of a number of newspapers about the lawsuit Alex had filed against the church. A yellow highlighter had been used to identify particular comments in the articles which were detrimental to the church. "I've got you!" Tommy said out loud.

Carefully Tommy sifted through the drawers and found the normal correspondence, bills, and notes to be found in any home office. Glancing through the bills, he found a utility bill addressed to Michael Lamb, not Vargas, at an address he did not recognize. He knew he could pull the address up on the GPS in the Navigator. The *alias has to be significant*, he thought. *"Lamb" as in the "Lamb of God."*

"Silk!" he yelled back to the bedrooms, "I think I know where he has her!"

Willis ran back into the living room and Tommy showed him what he had.

"That looks good, Tommy."

"Now how are we going to get out of here without setting off the alarm, Silk? We need to find and go to this address!"

Without any hesitation at all, Willis looked at Tommy and said simply, "We're going out the front door. Most alarms have a thirty or forty-five second delay so people can come in and deactivate the alarm before it goes off. By the time we get out of here and with your lead foot on the accelerator, we'll be long gone by the time it goes off."

Once again, Tommy thought as he drove out of the Heights with an alarm going off in the far distance, *Silk was right on the money!*

CHAPTER FORTY-FOUR

"Lieutenant Pierce," Tommy yelled into his cell phone, "This is Tommy O'Reilly. I think we've got him!"

Sam Pierce said calmly, "Settle down, Tommy. Tell me what you have."

"I've got a utility bill on an address for an individual named Michael Lamb, and it is being paid for by Michael Vargas. Don't you see the connection, Lieutenant? Michael Vargas … Michael Lamb … Lamb of God?"

"Give me the address, Tommy," Pierce calmly said, "and I will put you on hold."

Tommy did so, and seconds later Lieutenant Pierce came back on the phone. "It's a warehouse in Chinatown. I'll send a cruiser out there to see what they can spot. I want you to stay away, Tommy. I don't want you interfering with our officers!" Pierce said determinedly.

"Are you kidding? I have it on my GPS, and I'm heading there as we speak! I won't interfere with anybody, but I am going to be there," Tommy said, with just as much determination.

Pierce paused. "I can't order you not to, Tommy, but please don't do anything until the officers get there. They're trained for situations like this, and you're not. If she's there, you may wind up causing her harm if you interfere. Understand? I mean it Tommy, stay out of the way!"

As soon as Sam Pierce hung up the phone, without waiting for a response he called out to see if any task force units were in the vicinity of the address Tommy had given him.

"Lieutenant Pierce, this is Officer Nguyen. We're near the location you mentioned."

"There's a *possibility* that Aleksandra Kowalski might be at that location. Go to the location, run silent, no lights, no siren, and report back what you see or hear. Determine if there's any tangible evidence of her presence. There may be a civilian there, Tommy O'Reilly. Would you recognize him?"

"Yes, sir."

"Make sure he stays out of your way, and as soon as you have assessed the location, report back. Understood?" Lieutenant Pierce calmly ordered.

"Yes, sir."

Danh Nguyen was a twenty-year veteran of the Houston Police Department, and his partner tonight was Isaiah Jefferson, one year out of the police academy. It was a practice of the HPD to pair veterans with rookies so that the less experienced could learn something from the more experienced; sometimes it worked in reverse. Danh roared toward the location as instructed with no siren.

Tommy and Willis arrived at the address before Officers Nguyen and Jefferson. It was a metal building that appeared to be a warehouse. Tommy parked the Navigator and cautiously walked around and found a door on the east side of the warehouse. The steel door had a latch that was made for a padlock but was instead secured by a heavy chain slipped through the half-moon portion of the latch, and the chain was then padlocked. The chain and padlock looked fairly new and heavy enough not to be compromised unless cut with a heavy duty pair of shears. Further inspection of the half-moon-shaped latch indicated that the rivets attaching the latch to the door were old and rusted. Tommy thought he could possibly break the latch free from the building if he had a strong piece of metal to use as a lever to pry it off. He returned to the Navigator, found the tire iron, and returned to the building. Jamming the iron into the latch with one swift jerk, the latch popped off with the padlock and chain intact. It had been much easier than he had expected.

"How do you suppose he got in and locked the door from the outside?" Willis asked.

"Well, assuming that he's inside, there must be another door somewhere else. Come on, let's go inside," Tommy whispered.

"Are you sure? Maybe we should wait for the cops," Willis whispered back.

"Well, I'm going in. You can stay here if you want!" Tommy whispered with more determination.

Willis followed sheepishly as Tommy pulled open the heavy steel door and walked into the building. The warehouse was totally empty and dark except for the sunlight filtering through the open door, and it had an unusual odor that Tommy thought could be burning wax. In the dim light they saw something at the other end of the warehouse that looked like a box within the box of the warehouse. It looked like some kind of an office enclosure, and they saw that there was only a door to the office, no windows.

From behind they heard the crunch of gravel outside, which meant another car had just pulled into the small parking lot. As Tommy and Willis turned back toward the door to see who had just arrived, a shrill scream suddenly pierced the silence, a scream that neither of them would soon forget! It was the scream of a woman in absolute terror or pain. Briefly frozen in their tracks, they recovered and ran out and saw two men coming toward them. To their relief, it was two uniformed police officers who had just emerged from their HPD cruiser.

Tommy ran up to the older officer yelling, "Get a hold of Lieutenant Pierce immediately. We have the tangible evidence he needs. We both just heard a woman scream inside the warehouse, and it was the most horrific scream I've ever heard!"

"Okay, okay, settle down! You must be Mr. O'Reilly. I'm Officer Nguyen, and this is Officer Jefferson. Now please go over there and stand by your car and stay out of our way!" Officer Nguyen took out his phone and relayed the information to Lieutenant Pierce.

"Sounds like the tangible evidence we need," said Lieutenant Pierce his voice crackling over the speaker, "and since O'Reilly told you what happened, I'll vouch for him as the affiant. I'll get a search warrant and get right back to you."

Officer Nguyen turned to O'Reilly and said, "Lieutenant Pierce is in the process of obtaining a search warrant, and it shouldn't take too long. Once again, Mr. O'Reilly, you and your associate just stay put by your vehicle while we wait for Lieutenant Pierce's call with the warrant."

The two officers stood by the door, one with his weapon drawn, the other shining a flashlight into the empty darkness. They could see the office enclosure at the end of the warehouse. Minutes had passed since the conversation with Lieutenant Pierce, and then another desperate scream erupted from inside the cubicle echoing off the walls of the empty warehouse. "Let's get into that office or whatever it is, now, Nguyen!" Nguyen's partner shouted.

"No, we'll wait for the warrant, but go get the battering ram out of the car!" snapped Nguyen.

Officer Jefferson returned with the battering ram with Tommy and Willis inching up right behind him in total disregard of their previous instructions to stay put by their car. By the time they all reached Officer Nguyen, they could hear Lieutenant Pierce's voice resonating over the phone, "I have the search warrant, Nguyen, proceed. You're good to go! I have backup units and medical assistance on the way!"

Like a charging bull, Officer Jefferson rushed into the warehouse with Nguyen right behind him, followed closely by Tommy and Willis. When they reached the office, Jefferson heaved forward with the battering ram and slammed into the door. With a crack, the door tore from its hinges and hurled forward. The two officers started through the door as Nguyen, with his hand outstretched palm forward, cautioned Tommy and Willis, "You two stay here!"

As the two officers charged in, Tommy waited a moment and then flashed a look at Willis and said, "I don't know about you, Silk, but I'm going in!"

CHAPTER FORTY-FIVE

The two officers burst into the room with their weapons drawn, but they were momentarily disoriented by a glowing horizon of candles that filled the stale air with a musky odor. Tommy and Willis stumbled in behind them, squinting to adjust their eyes to the flickering light. Beyond the eerie glare they saw movement, a silhouette of a large, black-robed figure who seemed startled by their unwelcome entry. Another figure in a contorted position appeared to be a woman, bent forward with her head on a piece of wood exposing her neck and with her wrists shackled. Responding to the intruders, the large black-robed figure flung a leather whip aside and grabbed a large curved saber and screamed, "This heretic has still not confessed her sins but it doesn't matter!" As he gripped the shining saber with both hands and thrust it above his head, he cried, "God's will be done!"

"We're the police! Stop or we'll shoot!" Officer Nguyen had not even finished his warning when a deafening shot rang out, and the smell of cordite filled the air. As the powerful man was bringing down his sword toward the woman's exposed neck, he suddenly collapsed, as if his legs had been violently pulled out from under him. With a loud crack and the ping of metal hitting the hard wood contraption, the sword was released from the big man's hands as he fell writhing to the floor. The weapon had missed her head only by inches. Her soft rhythmic sobs had been muffled until now, but they were again drowned out by Officer Nguyen's orders.

"Don't move!" he shouted to the flailing figure on the concrete floor, but the man was apparently in so much pain he was flopping like a fish.

"Don't move!" Nguyen yelled again, but the man was unable to lie still. "Cover him, Jefferson, while I cuff him."

As he pulled the man's wrists out to put on the handcuffs he said, "You are under arrest. You have the right to remain silent…"

After he had completed the Miranda Rights and had closed the handcuffs on the man's wrists, he looked to see where Jefferson had shot him. Blood was rhythmically pulsing from the big man's knee. In the situation they had just faced, there were only two shots that would have immediately brought him down and prevented him from cleanly completing his down stroke to the target, a head shot or shot to the kneecap. Any other hit to the body, and he probably could have completed his downswing. While Nguyen had been wasting time with his useless warning, Jefferson had acted and chosen to shoot the kneecap, the harder of the two shots. *This rookie is good,* Nguyen thought and hoped Jefferson wouldn't live to regret not taking the head shot and killing him.

When Tommy ran into the room, a shot rang out that caused an intense ringing in his ears. *Please don't let that be Alex!* he thought to himself. He saw Nguyen and Jefferson rushing to a large man writhing on the floor. *That has to be Vargas,* he thought. He turned to the right and saw Alex bent forward with her arms and legs in some kind of trap. Even in the dim candlelight he could see her back was covered in blood. He rushed toward her, and when he reached her, he bent low and said, "Alex! Alex, can you hear me?"

She didn't move, so he bent closer and said louder, "Alex, can you hear me!"

She stirred, and Tommy said even louder, "Alex, are you all right?"

"Mr. O'Reilly," she gasped. "Mr. O'Reilly, you're here!"

"Yes, Alex, I'm here," he said gently. "And more help is on the way. You're going to be okay."

"Oh, thank God, Mr. O'Reilly. Thank God!" Alex croaked.

"Yes, Alex, I agree with you; thank God," Tommy quietly replied.

And then he looked at the big man groaning and twisting on the floor. The loathing he immediately felt displaced any further thoughts about God.

CHAPTER FORTY-SIX

The paramedics were very careful with Alex as they loaded her face down on an ambulance gurney. They had ignored the bleeding and handcuffed man on the floor. The next crew could take care of him.

"Where are you taking her?" Tommy asked.

"Mercy Hospital," one of the emergency technicians said. "Now please, sir, get out of the way!"

Tommy stepped out of the way and said, "I'll meet you there!"

Tommy and Willis ran out to the parking lot and saw that more HPD units had already arrived, and officers were racing opposite them to go into the building. Another ambulance also was pulling into the lot. Tommy and Willis jumped into the Navigator and sped off while Tommy opened his cell phone and hit speed dial.

"Hello, Tommy, what's a news magnet like you calling me for?"

Without any preamble whatsoever, Tommy blurted, "Don, we've found Aleksandra Kowalski, and she's in very bad shape."

"Where are they taking her?" he said in a tone that had become instantaneously serious.

"Mercy Hospital!" Tommy said quickly.

"I'll be there as soon as I can!" Don said and hung up immediately.

Don Erwin had been the right tackle on the U of H football team and was a bear of a man. Don had studied pre-med and had followed up with a degree from the UT Medical School. Don was one of the preeminent surgeons in Houston, if not in Texas; he and his wife Malone were among Tommy's best friends. Tommy knew Alex would be in the best of hands with Don calling the shots.

Tommy pulled into the ER entrance and parked in a no parking zone. "Silk, get in the driver's seat and stay here! Don't let anyone move you! I'll be right back!"

Tommy ran into the ER and asked for the nurse in charge. When a slightly built attractive woman came up to Tommy, he said, "I'm Tommy O'Reilly. The paramedics are bringing in Aleksandra Kowalski, and she's hurt badly. Doctor Don Erwin will be here very shortly, and I want him to be in charge of her triage and then her ultimate care. Are there any questions?"

The nurse in charge puffed to her full height and angrily said, "Yes, Mr. O'Reilly, I have questions! No one comes in here and tells us what to do. First of all, we have our own staff, and they're quite capable of taking care of a patient, regardless of her situation. Second, we will need proof of payment. How will that be handled?"

Tommy reached into his pocket, pulled out a billfold, and took out a credit card and then stared at the nurse until she began to shrink back. "This is a black American Express card. Do you know what that means?" She nodded. He continued, "I and this credit card are your proof of payment. Agreed?" Again she nodded. "Secondly, Don Erwin is in charge. He's the best surgeon in Houston. Do you know who he is?" Again she nodded in agreement. "He will decide who on your staff is capable of handling the situation, and if not, he'll bring in those he feels are capable, no matter what the costs. Agreed?"

"Yes, Mr. O'Reilly."

As Tommy turned around to leave, Alex was being wheeled in by the paramedics on a gurney. She was still on her stomach and blood had begun to seep through the sheet that covered her back. He turned to the nurse, and regretting his previous outburst said somberly, "That is Miss Kowalski." He looked at her name tag that said "Ruth Romero" and continued, "Nurse Romero, please take care of her until Dr Erwin gets here. Will you please do that?"

"Get out of my way, Mr. O'Reilly. I have work to do, and despite what you might think, we *do* know what we are doing *here!*" Nurse Romero said angrily as she brushed past him.

As Tommy got back into the truck he said, "Any problems, Silk?"

"None whatsoever. What about in there?" Willis asked back.

"No, no problems, Silk. I just had to deal with some minor insurance issues."

CHAPTER FORTY-SEVEN

"All rise," the bailiff said the next morning as Judge Bateman entered the courtroom and ascended the steps to his bench. "Please be seated," Judge Bateman said.

Tommy was glad there was one fewer member of the press corps seated behind him. Judge Bateman asked the bailiff to bring in the jury, and after they were seated in the jury box, he said, "I know I admonished you not to watch news reports about the trial, but I'm going to assume you have somehow heard that the plaintiff, Aleksandra Kowalski, was missing. I'm pleased to tell you she's been found."

Some of the jurors looked at one another and smiled.

"The man who abducted her was a psychotic individual who had no affiliation with anyone involved in this lawsuit, including the defendants or the Catholic Church. Do you understand this? If so, please say yes."

"Yes, Your Honor," the six jurors nodded and responded.

"However, she will not be available today in court," Judge Bateman continued. "This, again, is not a reflection on the Catholic Church or the defendants. Do you understand this? Again if you do, please say yes."

"Yes, Your Honor," they responded.

"Very well. Now we begin the closing argument. The plaintiff's counsel, Mr. O'Reilly, will first argue how he believes the testimony you have heard is relevant to the position of his client. Next, the defendants' counsel, Monsignor Renzulli, will argue how the testimony is relevant to the position of his clients. Then I will give you certain instructions, and you will retire to the jury room to consider answers to the questions I'll also give you. You'll select a foreman or forewoman from among you to answer on behalf of all of you when you have reached a unanimous verdict. Does any one of you have any questions?"

When there were none, Judge Bateman said, "Mr. O'Reilly, you may now address the jury."

Tommy stood up and clasped his hands in front of him as he faced the jury. "Shortly, the six of you will go into the jury room and be asked to decide unanimously the answers to two questions. Do the defendants discriminate against Alexander Kowalski solely because of her gender by denying her the right to attend a seminary in their jurisdiction to study for the priesthood? If so, then you will have to answer the next question. Do the defendants have justifiable cause to exclude her because of her gender?

"Let's talk about the first question. You've heard sworn testimony that a candidate for the seminary and a candidate for the priesthood *must* be an unmarried male baptized in the Catholic Church. I submit that is discriminatory behavior on its face. Those qualifications *specifically exclude women regardless of merit!*

Tommy looked each juror one by one and continued, "You have heard sworn testimony that Aleksandra Kowalski has the qualifications to be a priest by Dr. Turner, who is one of the psychologists contracted by the defendants to verify the qualifications of the candidates for the seminary and priesthood. That's Aleksandra Kowalski the *person,* not the woman or the man, but the *person!* The only thing she lacks to be a priest in the eyes of the defendants is a penis. I repeat, that is the *only* thing she lacks, and that is the part of the anatomy that a priest is forbidden to use in a sexual way! It is clear she has been discriminated against solely because of her female gender.

"I will also point out that the defendants have ordained *married* males who obviously do not meet their own qualifications of an *unmarried* male. They claim they have special reasons for doing this, and yet when asked whether a female who falls within those special circumstances could be ordained as well, they answered no because she would be a woman! The defendants ordain men, married and unmarried, which is clear. They will not ordain a woman no matter what, and that is also clear. The defendants clearly undertake a discriminatory practice based solely upon the gender of the person, which is also clear.

"Now let's talk about the second question. Do the defendants have justifiable cause to exclude women, such as the plaintiff, from the seminary and the priesthood? The defendants claim that they have justifiable cause because Jesus Christ did not appoint a woman as one of his apostles, only men. It's their position that by not appointing a woman, Jesus meant to exclude women forever from the priesthood. In order for their argument to have any validity at all, the *only* reason, has to be that he meant by that one act of omission to forever prevent women from joining the priesthood.

"If there's any *other* reason that caused him to appoint men only, their argument fails. If there are three or four or even more reasons why he did not appoint a woman as an apostle…well, you can see the foundation upon which they have built their argument is built on sand. All you need to do is find *one* valid reason why he did not name a woman as an apostle other than the one they claim and their foundation crumbles. Unfortunately for them there are many *more* reasons than *one!*

"Let's take a look at the times and circumstances in which Jesus appointed his apostles. "Their number was twelve, and that number corresponded with the twelve tribes of Israel, as you have heard from the testimony. This was part of the Jewish tradition that Jesus of Nazareth was there to fulfill.

"You also heard there had never been a head of a tribe who was a woman, and to maintain that tradition, Jesus Christ would have appointed only men. That was the tradition, and that's what he would have done. Did he mean that men only were to be priests forever? Did he mean that with the passage of time and when his new religion expanded and broke from the Hebrew tradition, women were to be excluded *forever* from the priesthood? I don't think so. Once this initial and seemingly valid reason for appointing men no longer existed, what would have been the point?"

Tommy took some time to let his points sink in by pretending to look at his notes, then he looked up again and directed a sincere gaze to the jury. "There are other reasons why he might not have appointed a woman as an apostle. You have heard testimony that women at the time were little more than slaves. At the time of Jesus Christ, no woman could hold a leadership position, period! No how, no way!

"Jesus Christ was not on earth to undertake social reform. He didn't do that with slavery and other social norms that he disagreed with, and he didn't do it when he appointed only men as priests. Did he mean that would be the same forever? I don't think so. Once social customs evolved to accept women as equal to men, and this valid reason for appointing men no longer existed, what would have been the point?

"The apostles also had characteristics other than being of the male gender, such as being Jewish and married. The defendants dismiss these other characteristics as incidental and not fundamental. The defendants dismiss *any* characteristic that the apostles had except for one, their gender. They claim that these other characteristics were incidental in light of the social times in which Jesus lived. Yet they ignore the social custom of the taboo against women, which was very prevalent in those times. Are they talking out of both sides of their mouths? I'll let you answer that for yourselves.

"Let's talk about how being Jewish and married is incidental. Those characteristics seemed pretty fundamental to me. Ask yourselves about your own marital status and ethnic roots. They deal directly with your family and your family heritage! How fundamental are they to you? Can the defendants merely dismiss these as being incidental and not fundamental any more than gender is fundamental? I don't think so.

"The characteristics of the apostles were all the same. If any of them were fundamental, then they all had to be fundamental. If any of them were incidental, then they were all incidental. How can anyone two thousand years later pick and choose among the characteristics of the apostles and determine which Jesus meant to last *forever* and disregard the rest as incidental?"

"However, the characteristics were *all*, and I repeat, *all*, incidental to the times in which Jesus Christ lived. Nothing more, nothing less! He didn't mean that a priest should be Jewish forever! He didn't want to rock the boat of Jewish hierarchy by appointing a gentile at the time. And he did not mean that priests should be males forever! He didn't want to rock the boat of a male dominated society by appointing a woman at the time. Those characteristics and all the others common to the apostles were determined by and incidental to the customs of those times, nothing more and nothing less. *Just that!*" As time passed and those customs were no longer in existence, the characteristics required by those customs were no longer required. It's *foolish* and *unreasonable* to read anymore into it other than that.

"Now let's talk about the two different instances that women were present when both men and women received priestly powers from Jesus Christ: the Last Supper and the Pentecost. You heard testimony that says there is equal evidence to show that women were present on those occasions. If women were there, they received the same directions that the men did. If you believe what the defendants say, that Jesus Christ treated women equally with men, would he have excluded them from the Last Supper or the Pentecost?

"It doesn't sound like he would have. Jesus Christ wasn't around to run the early church after his death, and it seems clear that the men in control at that time would have excluded women from any leadership position because that's what *they* believed, not what *he* believed. I believe a strong case can be made that while Jesus Christ excluded women from the initial apostles for social reasons, that just before his death and after his resurrection he included them when he conferred the power of priesthood to his original twelve apostles.

"There is no scriptural evidence that says women were not there, and the actions of Jesus would indicate they most likely were. The defendants will say this is entirely supposition, and there is no direct biblical evidence for the claim. I respond that the defendant's proposition that Jesus intended to have men only in the priesthood forever is entirely supposition, and there is no direct biblical evidence for *that* claim."

Once more Tommy paused but continued looking at the jury. His gaze became more intense. "That brings me to my last point. You heard testimony that the dogma of the Catholic Church is the infallible truth, which the defendants hold dear. Catholics are forbidden to believe otherwise. One dogma is that men and women are created equal, and another is that only males can be priests. Those dogmas are in direct contradiction to each other, so which one should we believe? The first dogma follows what Jesus Christ said and did, and the second dogma is based upon what he didn't do."

Tommy put his hands in front of him, palms up, and began alternatively raising one and lowering the other as if they were a balancing scale. "Said and did … or did not do … did not do … or said and did. In resolving the conflict between the two, which one do you think he really meant? Which has the most weight? The one he taught—that men and women are equal in every respect? Or the one he didn't teach—that only a man can be a priest, and not a woman?"

Once again Tommy paused and looked each juror one at a time in the eyes and then said, "Ladies and gentlemen, I have been trying lawsuits for many years, and I have never seen anyone talk so much out of both sides of their mouth while under oath. They swear men and women are equal and then swear only men can be priests.

"That … just … doesn't … make … sense! They swear that only unmarried men can be ordained and then swear that they ordain married Episcopal priests. *That … .just … .doesn't … ..make … sense!* If their positions on those issues are so nonsensical, how can anyone possibly think they're right when they say what they do about a male-only priesthood?

"To summarize what I've said, the defendants would have you believe that they're justified in their discriminatory practices because Jesus did not do something, and therefore they shouldn't have to do it either, despite the harm it does to women."

"They say, 'We have looked back two thousand years and have concluded that of all the characteristics the apostles had, the only one which Jesus meant to last forever as a qualification for the priesthood is the male gender. All of the rest were incidental of the times and the fact he didn't appoint a women was not!' Well, certainly their reasoning on their fundamental qualification of a male having to be *unmarried* in order to be a priest hasn't been stellar. I submit that the same holds true for their exclusion of females!"

After a momentary pause he continued, "I believe the evidence is clear that you, in clear conscience, can only answer the first question, 'Do the defendants discriminate solely because of gender?' and that is with a resounding '*yes!*' I believe the evidence is also clear that you can only answer the second question, 'Do the defendants have reasonable and justifiable cause to discriminate?' and that is with a resounding '*no!*' There can be no other choice."

Tommy looked at them for a moment and then said quietly and sincerely, "I thank you, and most of all, Aleksandra Kowalski thanks you for your time and attention."

He turned and sat down to total and absolute silence.

CHAPTER FORTY-EIGHT

"Monsignor Renzulli, you may now address the jury," Judge Bateman said.

"Thank you, Your Honor," Renzulli said. Turning to the jury, he said, "And I also wish to thank you for your diligence and attention. When you retire to the jury room and address the questions put before you, the question you have to answer in your own mind is whether my clients, the Archdiocese of Galveston-Houston and Bishop Sierra, are arbitrary and capricious in what they do. In other words, are they *mean-spirited* people?

"Do they believe their activities are justified, or do they act out of hatred and disrespect for women? That's what discriminatory behavior is all about. It's a behavior born out of bias and prejudice that has no justifiable basis. In order for you to find for the plaintiff, you have to believe that the preponderance of the evidence conclusively shows my clients hate women and do not want them to be priests no matter what.

"I submit that's not what they believe, and that's not what the testimony shows they believe. The testimony shows without a doubt that the defendants justifiably believe that what they're doing is a direction from the example of Jesus Christ.

"Jesus Christ did not appoint a woman as an apostle. That is an indisputable fact! The twelve apostles were the first priests; there is no dispute about this. The church believes and the Scriptures show the apostles were ordained as priests at the Last Supper.

Counsel for the plaintiff suggests that women were also present at the Last Supper and that Jesus Christ granted the same ordination to the women who were there.

"I ask you, what women? What woman? Who were they, and where did they go? If any women had been ordained as priests, those women would have known that they were ordained as priests! The twelve apostles would also have known those women had been ordained as priests because the twelve were there also. Would those women have simply disappeared from the early church and the written Scriptures? Would the apostles have ignored and disregarded those women if Jesus had ordained them? No, I don't think so.

"There's no evidence to suggest that women were present, but we know one thing. The twelve apostles were there, and they were ordained by Jesus Christ, and all of them were men. That we know is true. That's the only thing about the Last Supper we know to be true!"

Renzulli waited a moment and then continued, "Plaintiff's counsel argues over and over that there is no direct revelation in the Scriptures that priests have to be men, and it is nonsense to rely on something Jesus didn't do and not do it forever. Is it really? Jesus didn't hurt others. That is something else he *didn't* do. Is it nonsense to think he wanted his followers to follow *that* example of not doing something forever? Of course it's not. To say a person can't set an example by *not* doing something . . . now that is nonsense."

Monsignor Renzulli paused and looked at each individual juror directly one by one. He had their attention, and he was making points. "Counsel for the plaintiff has suggested social norms would have dictated the selection of men by Jesus. I don't know whether you believe Jesus Christ was God-made man or not, but my clients do.

They believe that God, as man, could have appointed any woman he chose to be an apostle.

"The very definition of God is that he can do anything. Does anybody believe, for even one second, that God, with the unimaginable powers that only God can have, would be even minutely bothered by the social norms of the society? He could have easily appointed a woman but did not do so. The reason he did not do so was because he was establishing the basis of his future church on earth. Every *fundamental* thing Jesus did or refrained from doing is an example for all Christians to follow today. Not incidental things he did like appointing apostles that were married or had beards. The apostles also spoke Aramaic and were uneducated. Some of them were also fisherman, and some of them may have had red hair too. Who cares? Those were all incidental characteristics, and the plaintiff's counsel is trying to confuse you by saying all of those characteristics along with the apostles' gender are merely incidental. What can be more fundamental to any of us then our gender? *It is what defines us all!* It is as fundamental as one can get. He set fundamental examples in all ways, and the church tries to follow still today each and every one. That we know is true."

Renzulli paused to indicate a change of thought for effect and continued. "The first apostles knew Jesus as well as you would know anyone with whom you lived for *three* years. They ate with him, slept in the same house with him, talked to and listened to him, were constantly with him for three whole years. Think about it. That is a long time.

"Ask yourselves, how well would you know someone if you did what they did with Jesus for three years? The answer is obvious. You would know him very, very well. After his death when they had an opportunity to select another apostle, and when they had many highly qualified women to call upon, they chose a man who may not have even known Jesus Christ. The first mention of him in the Scriptures is when he is appointed to replace Judas.

"The apostles, of all people, would have known what Jesus Christ would have wanted. They were tortured in horrible, unimaginable ways and murdered for doing what they knew Jesus Christ wanted them to do. To think that they would have not done what he wanted because of a social norm? Preposterous! I don't believe it, and neither should you. Forget social norms of the time and any bias the apostles might have had against women, as plaintiff's counsel suggests. If Jesus Christ would have wanted it, they would have *known* it, and they would have *done* it!

"In the two thousand years since the time of Jesus, there have certainly been hundreds of thousands, maybe a million or more, of Catholic clergy who were and are now dedicated to doing Christ's work on earth. That's their only mission and goal in life. No wife, no children, no other pursuits to interfere with their focus. Their job is literally their life.

"Throughout history since the time of Jesus they have asked themselves many times the question that you are being asked to answer today. What was the will of Jesus? They have concluded absolutely that the Catholic Church is justified in excluding women from the priesthood. It would have been much easier to answer differently. They wouldn't have the controversy they have today. But they didn't. They have prayed about it, researched it, discussed it, and looked at it in every way possible. They have consistently answered it as Christ would have wanted them to answer it. The priesthood is to forever be reserved for the male gender only.

There has been no inconsistency in this teaching for two thousand years. That is something else we also know to be true.

"Now I get to the question I raised when I first started. Each one of you must ask yourself, 'Are my clients, the archdiocese and Bishop Sierra, doing this arbitrarily without regard to anything other than their hatred and disrespect for women?' You met Bishop Sierra. Ask yourself, 'Is he sincere in not allowing women to the seminary out of good faith or is he just a mean guy who hates women?'" There were a few smiles from the jurors. Pausing, he said "Remember, It doesn't matter that you believe what Catholics believe. It doesn't matter at all!"

"Counsel for the plaintiff bases his entire case on the position that the defendants should not believe as they believe. He's put a lot of smoke out there about reasons for what Jesus might or might not have done. That's absolutely of no relevance whatsoever! It doesn't matter what others might believe or might not believe. What is relevant, and this is extremely important for you to understand, is whether my clients have justifiable reasons to believe the way *they* believe, and therefore act as they act?

"I believe the answer is obvious. My clients have determined that what they do is what is required of them by their faith and belief, and they cannot do otherwise. It's *a justifiable* belief that causes their activities. It's simply not true that they act arbitrarily and capriciously out of disrespect for women. They have just cause and a reasonable basis for limiting the priesthood to males. That's the only answer possible under the preponderance of the evidence. It unquestionably leads you to the one and only answer to the second jury question, '*yes!*'"

Monsignor Renzulli stared at the jury for a moment, and they stared back, lost in thought. He slowly turned and sat down, and again there was absolute silence in the courtroom.

CHAPTER FORTY-NINE

Waiting on a jury was the hardest thing Tommy had to do in his life. It was always hard, and he knew he could never get used to it. The judge had retired to his chambers, using that time to catch up on the usual things that needed be done. But the parties and counsel had nothing to do but sit and wait. It was a total feeling of helplessness, and Tommy did not like being helpless. Some counsel read books and novels to pass the time. Tommy thought that was a waste of time. Some counsel sat and thought back over the trial regretting things they had done or wishing they had done things they didn't do. Tommy thought that was a bigger waste of time. He remembered Joe Bob used to go to Paddy's to wait for the call that the jury had reached a verdict and drink scotch in the meantime. But Paddy's was long gone, and Tommy didn't drink during the day anyway. So Tommy and Willis just sat and waited … and waited.

The bailiff entered the courtroom and announced, "The jury has reached a verdict. I'll get Judge Bateman."

Tommy glanced at his watch and noticed it had been five hours and thirty-six minutes since the jury had retired to discuss the verdict. That was a long time for two jury questions, the first one being an obvious yes, or so Tommy thought. The lion's share of the time was focused on the second question, "Do they have justifiable cause to exclude women from the seminary and priesthood?" It must have been the two women against the Catholic man, two against one, but men by nature were more aggressive.

Tommy wondered who won out and swayed the other side and the other three men. Whoever they selected as the foreman might give him a clue. He could also tell by who the jurors looked at when they came back into the jury box. If they looked at him and smiled, he was in. If they looked at Monsignor Renzulli and smiled, he would be in deep trouble.

The bailiff brought the jury in and seated them in the jury box. The jurors alternately looked at him and Monsignor Renzulli with no emotion. No clue whatsoever. Everyone was seated when the bailiff announced, "All rise," and Judge Bateman once again walked the steps to the bench for the last time in this lawsuit.

"Ladies and gentlemen of the jury, have you reached a verdict?" Judge Bateman asked.

"We have, Your Honor," said Mr. Madapusi, and he stood up. The other five jurors had selected the Hindu as the foreman. The foreman was typically elected because he or she had been a forcible presence in the jury room. Tommy was somewhat surprised, and then he remembered that he and Silk had forgotten to research the Hindu beliefs.

"Will the bailiff please bring me the written verdict of the jury?" requested Judge Bateman. After he received it, he read it without any emotion. Then he turned to the jury and asked the foreman, "Is this the unanimous verdict of the jury?"

"Yes, Your Honor," Mr. Madapusi answered, nodding his head.

Judge Bateman continued, "Concerning question number one, do you find that the defendants discriminate against women solely because of their gender by excluding them from the seminary in order to study for the Catholic priesthood? Yes or no? What is your answer?"

Mr. Madapusi replied, "Our answer to that question is yes, Your Honor. They discriminate against women solely because of their gender."

No surprise there, Tommy thought.

"Since you've answered question number one in the affirmative, you are required to answer question number two. Do you find the defendants have a justifiable basis to exclude women from the seminary in order to study for the Catholic priesthood solely because of their gender? Yes or no? What is your answer?"

Mr. Madapusi took a few moments and looked at his jury form, and the silence was stifling in the courtroom. Not a cough, not a shuffle of the feet, no sounds whatsoever. Then he looked up and stared straight at Tommy O'Reilly and said, "Our answer to that question is … no, Your Honor. They do not have a justifiable basis."

And the courtroom erupted.

CHAPTER FIFTY

As Manuel pulled into the drop-off area at Mercy Hospital and Tommy stepped out of the car, he said, "Stay close by, Manny. I'll call you on the cell phone when I need you to pick me up, and I shouldn't be long."

Tommy went inside and took the elevator to the floor with the intensive care unit. He went to the desk just outside of the ICU and asked which room Aleksandra Kowalski was in. The nurse told him, "She, as all other patients in the ICU, is only allowed family as visitors. Are you a member of the family?"

"No, but Dr. Erwin should have left my name as a permitted visitor."

She shuffled through some papers until she found the one she wanted and looked up at him. "What is your name?"

After looking at her name he said softly, "I'm Tommy O'Reilly, Nurse Wilkinson."

"I thought that was you, Mr. O'Reilly, but I have to make certain. Do you have identification?" the nurse asked back.

Tommy showed her his driver's license and she said, "Yes, Mr. O'Reilly, you are on the list. She is in 3D, but please be quiet, and if she's asleep, please don't wake her up."

"Yes, ma'am," Tommy said and walked down the hall to 3D. There was a policeman seated in a chair outside her door reading a magazine. He looked up as Tommy approached and nodded at him. Tommy nodded back and pushed the door open as quietly as he could. He noticed Alex was lying prone face down on the bed. *The wounds to her back will take a lot of time to heal,* Tommy thought. He approached the bed and spoke quietly. "Alex?"

She opened her eyes and looked at him and mumbled drowsily, "Mr. O'Reilly, you're here. Is the trial over?"

"Yes, Alex, the trial is over," Tommy replied softly.

More alert because of Tommy's answer, she raised her head slightly and asked, "What did the jury say?"

Tommy thought a moment and then said, "The jury said that the defendants did not have a justifiable basis to exclude you from the seminary."

"Thank God, Mr. O'Reilly," Alex said, lying her head back down. "Then we were right?"

"Yes, Alex, *we* were right," Tommy replied.

"So I can start into the seminary at the start of the next semester, assuming I'm well?" Alex asked earnestly.

Tommy looked out the window at the western setting sun and thought it had been a long day. Turning back to Alex, he quietly said, "No, Alex, you can't start the seminary as soon as you're well."

"Why not?" she asked, leaning up slightly again, totally confused.

Tommy looked back at Alex with a calmness that he did not feel. "As you know, there were essentially three issues we had to win in order to force the defendants to accept you to the seminary.

"First, the jury had to find that the defendants excluded you from the seminary solely because of your gender. If the jury had found that the defendants did not do that, that would have been it, and the trial would have been over. The jury found that the defendants did exclude you solely because of your gender, and that took us to the second issue.

"The second issue was for the jury to determine whether the defendants have a reasonable basis to exclude you. If the jury had answered that question yes, the defendants have a reasonable basis to exclude you, then the trial would've been over. They answered the question no. The defendants did not have a reasonable basis to exclude you, so that took us to the third issue.

"The third issue left it to Judge Bateman to decide whether or not to grant a mandatory injunction to require them to accept you. A mandatory injunction is available when the plaintiff, which is you, has no other adequate remedies available. I argued that the Catholic Church believes they're the original church that Jesus established. Bishop Sierra testified that the Catholic Church is the one and only true church, and I argued that would be the only available remedy for you as a Catholic in order to become a priest.

"Monsignor Renzulli argued that there were many other Christian faiths that accepted women to their seminaries to study for the priesthood, and your own testimony supported that. Therefore, he argued, there are a number of other remedies available to you in order for you to become a priest in a Christian religion other than Catholic." Tommy again looked out the window and noticed the sun had finished its journey of the day and was below the horizon.

After a moment, he turned back to Alex and continued, "When Judge Bateman rendered his decision, he said, 'If one believes in God, then by the very definition of God there can only be one God... *only one.*' Then he said, 'If one believes that Jesus Christ was the son of God, then there can only be one Jesus Christ... *only one.*'"

Tommy paused again and thought, *This might be the hardest conversation I've ever had as an attorney.* He continued, "Judge Bateman went on to say, 'If anyone is a Christian and worships Jesus Christ, then the only object of that worship is the *same* God-made man. All Christian denominations, even though they may do it in a different way, have by definition to worship the same Jesus Christ. There is only one.'"

Tommy looked at Alex softly and continued, "Judge Bateman concluded his ruling by saying that if you wished to become a priest in a Christian religion there were any number of them that would accept you. Since you have other remedies available to you, he found that a mandatory injunction was not available to you under the law. The short story is he bought Renzulli's argument and not mine. I'm sorry Alex. That's why you won't be able to go to the seminary. Judge Bateman did not order them to accept you."

For a long few moments, Alex looked at Tommy with those unbelievable emerald eyes and then said, "We were right, Mr. O'Reilly. We were right! The jury said so! Someday the Catholic Church will just have to accept women to the priesthood. They'll just have to, won't they?!"

Tommy thought a moment and then said, "Yes, Alex, someday, but not today." And he turned and quietly walked out the door.

EPILOGUE

It was the first part of July, and Tommy was in his office. In honor of the upcoming Fourth of July, Tommy had chosen a blue seersucker suit with a white shirt and a red, white, and blue striped tie. He was sitting in his chair looking out the window of his office with his burgundy alligator boots propped up on his desk. This was a double-ninety-five day as Tommy called them, ninety-five degrees temperature and ninety-five degrees humidity. The air was so thick Tommy thought he could see it, cut it, and serve it on a plate. It was the type of day that if it happened every day of the year instead of only 140 days a year, the city fathers of Houston couldn't give the place away.

Alexander Kowalski had recovered from the wounds she had received from Michael Vargas and had become a media darling. A number of Christian churches had contacted her to become a priest in their congregations. The Episcopal bishop in Houston had won her over by pointing out that the Episcopal religion was exactly like the Catholic religion except for their allegiance to the pope and the dogma of male-only priests. After due consideration, she had agreed that the Episcopal bishop was right. She told him that she was ready to accept that faith and undertake the education required to become an

Episcopal priest. Her decision was accompanied by a press conference and great fanfare. The last time Tommy talked to her, he thought she seemed happy.

Michael Vargas had been charged with kidnapping, assault and battery, and attempted murder. His attorney had pled not guilty by reason of insanity. Not only had Vargas's psychiatrists testified that the defendant did not know the difference between what was right and what was wrong at the time of his crime, the state's psychiatrist had agreed with his opinion as well. The psychiatrists believed Vargas *still* felt he was right and had no remorse whatsoever. The judge of the criminal district court that had been assigned Vargas's case had no choice but to send Vargas to the state mental hospital until such time as he was declared legally sane.

The judge, the prosecutors, and even Vargas's attorney knew that it was only a matter of time, with the drugs he would receive and the counseling he would get, that he would be declared sane and walk out. Any smart guy could con the system, and from the smile on Vargas's face as he walked out of that criminal courtroom, he knew he would not be incarcerated very long. As officers Nguyen and Jefferson left the courtroom, Jefferson turned to Nguyen and said, "I should have taken the head shot."

Tommy had talked to Nikki Butler once since that Saturday night in his apartment. She told him that she needed time to think about what they had discussed that night and whether he was a person she wanted to continue to spend time with. She assured him that she would call him after she thought it over. Since enough time had passed for Nikki to read *War and Peace* three times over, he thought "call Tommy" was not on her to do list.

After his Saturday discussion with Luisa about Aleksandra Kowalski, he drove out the following Saturday for his weekly visit. His mother had left word with the attendant at the desk that she didn't wish to see him. He had tried to call her a number of times, but she had him on her no-call list. Tommy did something he had never done before. He actually wrote a letter to his mother in his own hand explaining his reasons for what he had done. It was returned to him unopened. He tried again with the same result. His mother would not respond, and there was nothing he could do. It bothered him a lot. They were all each other had, mother and son. Unless she relented, she would die alone in a home for the elderly. It made no sense and worse, he couldn't change it.

As Tommy turned from the window and his reverie, he looked at the top of his desk and saw the "last straw." He had read the letter twice and decided to read it again. It was a letter of *Latae Sententiare* explaining his excommunication from the Catholic Church. Tommy had looked up the Latin term and found it meant "sentence already passed." The letter was signed by Bishop Cardinal Sierra.

The letter said there were eight instances where a person might incur excommunication *Latae Sententiare,* one of them being heresy. Tommy's works and deeds had been verified to be heretical against one of the sacred dogmas of the Catholic Church, the right of the Catholic Church to reserve the priesthood of the Catholic Church to the male gender only. As a result of his heresy, Tommy was no longer eligible to participate in the sacraments administered by the Catholic Church. He was also forbidden to enter a Catholic Church until such time as he took the Sacrament of Reconciliation, confessed his sins of heresy, and executed a statement of repentance. If he decided to do this, then all of the required actions had to be done with the Archbishop of the Archdiocese of Galveston-Houston as his confessor. The Archbishop of the Archdiocese of Galveston-Houston had solely reserved the right to decide whether Tommy could ever be reinstated to the Communion of the Faithful.

The first time Tommy read the letter, it made him mad. The second time he became incensed, and now he was livid. He had been right, and Renzulli and Sierra were wrong. The jury had unanimously said so! They said the church doctrine against women as priests had no reasonable basis. How could Sierra arbitrarily deny him the right to practice his Catholic religion without due process? The fact he had seldom chosen to do so was not the issue. The issue was that he had the right to do so! The First Amendment guaranteed him the right to the freedom of his religion and allowed him to worship as he pleased. It was a constitutional right! They were violating the same First Amendment that Renzulli and Sierra had tried to use against him. Could he bring a lawsuit against them, and could he use his First Amendment rights against them to overthrow his excommunication? The more he thought about it, the more it made sense.

"Silk!" he yelled. "Come in here! I've got an idea!"

AUTHOR'S NOTE

The book you have just read is a work of fiction, nothing more, and nothing less. In the interest of the story, I took a few liberties with some federal procedural and statutory law. However, concerning the arguments for and against the ordination of women in the Catholic Church, I attempted, to the best of my ability, to portray each one in the most objective way I could.

In July of 2010 the head of the Roman Catholic Church, Pope Benedict XVI, revised the Catholic Church's ecclesiastical laws and strengthened its in-house rules on sex abuse cases. But in doing so he also ruled that any priest caught ordaining women would be designated as having committed a *grave crime*. This is the same term used for a priest who engages in pedophilia.

While reasonable people could debate whether the horrors of pedophilia and the ordination of a female priest belong in the same category of an offense, what is clear and obvious by making the comparison is that this pope and the present hierarchy of the Catholic Church is intractable on whether women can be priests.

What few polls that have been taken of American Catholics about the issue have resulted in an almost even split. It is a highly charged topic in the United States today with no room for compromise of opinions. However the Catholic Church is not an institution of the people, by the people, or for the people since the Catholic Church is not a democracy but an autocracy, albeit a benevolent one. As such, it appears highly unlikely that the Holy See will ever be influenced by the opinion of one, some, or all of the one billion Catholics in the world.

I hope you enjoyed the story.

—R.A. Brown

e|LIVE

listen|imagine|view|experience

AUDIO BOOK DOWNLOAD INCLUDED WITH THIS BOOK!

In your hands you hold a complete digital entertainment package. In addition to the paper version, you receive a free download of the audio version of this book. Simply use the code listed below when visiting our website. Once downloaded to your computer, you can listen to the book through your computer's speakers, burn it to an audio CD or save the file to your portable music device (such as Apple's popular iPod) and listen on the go!

How to get your free audio book digital download:

1. Visit www.tatepublishing.com and click on the e|LIVE logo on the home page.
2. Enter the following coupon code:
   fc0f-6675-99e4-81c3-f60c-6437-a2f8-4b6a
3. Download the audio book from your e|LIVE digital locker and begin enjoying your new digital entertainment package today!